BEIGE

EIGE

cecil castellucci

CANDLEWICK PRESS
CAMBRIDGE, MASSACHUSETTS

Copyright © 2007 by Cecil Castellucci

First edition 2007

Library of Congress Cataloging-in-Publication Data
Castellucci, Cecil, date.
Beige / Cecil Castellucci. — 1st U.S. ed.
p. cm.
Summary: Katy, a quiet French Canadian teenager, reluctantly
leaves Montréal to spend time with her estranged father,
an aging Los Angeles punk rock legend.
ISBN 978-0-7636-3066-9
[1. Fathers and daughters—Fiction. 2. Punk rock music—Fiction.
3. Musicians—Fiction. 4. Self-perception—Fiction.
5. Los Angeles (Calif.)—Fiction.] I. Title.
PZ7.C26865Be 2007
[Fic]—dc22 2006052458

2 4 6 8 10 9 7 5 3 1

Printed in the United States of America

This book was typeset in Galliard.

Candlewick Press
2067 Massachusetts Avenue
Cambridge, Massachusetts 02140

visit us at www.candlewick.com

To all you dirty rats. I love you.

LOS ANGELES

X

The first thing I notice as the plane lands at LAX is that it is cloudy and pouring rain. So much for the myth that it's always sunny in Los Angeles.

Never mind. The weather matches my mood, though on the outside I am all clear skies and sunshine.

I *smile*. Even though I have to wear an embarrassing Air Canada Unaccompanied Minor baseball hat and a big lanyard around my neck holding a card with my name and address written on it like I'm a six-year-old who might get lost on a school field trip. Even though as I get off the airplane, I am escorted to baggage claim by an overly perky and way-too-in-my-business flight attendant named Candy.

I wish she could just break the rules. I wish she could just leave me alone to face the embarrassment that is my father.

"The Rat will pick you up at the airport, Katy," Mom said when I left Montréal, and I almost thought I heard her say under her breath, *"J'espère."*

I hope.

"Do you see him?" Candy asks, smiling at me. Big teeth. I'm glad to see there is a sesame seed stuck in one of them. I wish a cavity on her while I smile sweetly.

My eyes scan the baggage claim area. Any number of the men standing around looking eagerly like they are waiting for someone could be The Rat. I almost don't want to find him, like maybe it would be best for everyone involved if he just forgot to show up. From what I know of him, that could happen. That's not even stretching my imagination. If he didn't show up, I could just shrug, say I tried, and go to Peru.

I size up this one older guy. He's distinguished-looking, wearing a button-down green oxford shirt and khaki pants. The man looks like he's wearing his Sunday-best-trying-to-impress, like a cleaned-up version of the last picture I have of The Rat. He could be The Rat. Sort of. If I squint. I am almost relieved. I could maybe hang with this guy for two and a half weeks. *Maybe*. I start to make my way toward him. But then someone else catches my eye and my heart sinks.

"Yeah," I say to Candy. "I see him."

Everybody sees him.

The Rat is six feet five inches tall and wears a tiny cowboy hat on his head. He's got a rolled-up cigarette (I hope not a joint) hanging out of his mouth, and his skinny sleeve-tattooed arms poke out of his once black, now faded gray T-shirt that says NOSTRA DUMB ASS. He is scruffy, greasy, unshaven, and probably unwashed. His pegged jeans are dingy and look like he wears them every single day.

My father, Beau Ratner, punk name The Rat, looks just like a bum.

As soon as he sees me, he stands up on the edge of the baggage claim belt, throws his hands in the air, waves them around, and yells, "Hellllooooooooooo, Katy!"

Some people look at him and laugh.

Some people are irritated.

Some people follow The Rat's laughing eyes straight to me.

Someone please throw a pail of water on me so I can melt right into the ground like the Wicked Witch of the West.

Candy goes over to The Rat and signs me over to him. Transaction complete.

I wish I'd grabbed my receipt release form right out of her hand. I was close enough. I could've made a break for it. I could've hopped on a plane going anywhere. Out of *here*. I think about moving fast. I think about running for the double doors and pushing people out of the way. I think about just disappearing.

Am I doing it? I check my surroundings. No. I'm still standing in place with a smile on my face. I even lift my hand and make a little wave hello to The Rat, which makes him take his mini cowboy hat and swing it around his head.

I should have spoken up. I will never ever understand why Mom wouldn't let me accompany her on the archaeological expedition to Peru. I should have outlined an argument to her that it would have been much more educational there than two and a half weeks in Los Angeles. I could have helped her finish her PhD thesis. I could have made a history-altering discovery. I could have seen Machu Picchu!

Usually, she takes me everywhere, even research trips. Usually, she lets me sit at the adult table. Usually, she lets me participate in everything. She is patient with my questions and giving with her time. In all my life Mom and I have never been apart for more than a few days.

We're a team.

But this time, the site was too remote. This time it just wasn't going to work out. This time she was just going to go by herself. This time it was just easier that way. This time I would be in the way. This time she would get more done if I weren't there.

I know how to be quiet. I would've stayed out of her way. I've done it a million times before. She knows that. That's one of the things she loves about me.

Now I have to be without her for a whole *two and a half weeks*.

"It's going to be hard for me, too, Katy," she

said while she was packing her bags, but I could see that really, she was excited. Her thoughts were already in the Andes uncovering the secrets of the Incas. She was already living there without me.

"Think of it as an adventure," she said. "Think about how much we'll have to share with each other when we get back."

The difference is that Mom is visiting the *Andes* and I'm in Los Angeles with a man everyone calls *the rat.*

I want to frown. I try. I try to grimace, but instead, my smile just gets wider.

An alarm signals and the suitcases start to spit out onto the spinning conveyor belt. The Rat jumps off the belt and runs toward me and swoops me up into a back-cracking bear hug.

"Look at you! Look at you! You're huge!" he says. "I can't believe how much you've grown. I mean, of course I've seen the pictures. But now you're here! In the flesh!"

The Rat is all bending and hugging me, and I am as stiff as a board. I can't relax. It doesn't feel natural. I want to remind him that he's not anything to me that I would call *Dad*. He hasn't even come to visit me in Canada since I was seven years old. I want to remind him that to me he is just e-mails, phone calls, some letters, and a bunch of awkward presents.

"Your guitar will probably be with the over-sized luggage," he says. "I'll go pick it up while you watch for your bags."

He rushes over to get the guitar that I didn't ask for and didn't need. I definitely didn't want to bring it with me to California. But Mom insisted.

"Music is his life," she always says with a smile that looks like a secret.

"His life," I remind her. "Not mine."

The Rat has been the drummer in about a million bands, but he's best known for being in a band called Suck.

I might not *know* music, I might not *like* music, but everyone with half a brain knows the band Suck. They were never famous. They were more like *infamous*. Infamously un-famous. Infamously messed up. Infamously the greatest band that never made it.

I have tried to listen to the seven-inch vinyls my mom swears are classics. I have tried to listen to the CD reissue of their out-of-print first (and only) full-length record. Nails on a chalkboard sound more pleasing.

But no matter how much I protested, the guitar, a purple acoustic/electric Daisy Rock guitar, a present for my thirteenth birthday, had to come with me to California.

I have taken it out of its case exactly three times. Mom always says you should try something truly and completely before you give it up. She knows of what she speaks, though perhaps in her day she has taken that idea a bit too far. But it's a good point. It's following an academic line of inquiry.

I, myself, discovered that I feel about the guitar the way I feel about eating eel. I knew I wouldn't like it as soon as I set my eyes on it. Trying it didn't change anything.

It didn't matter. She wouldn't budge. She insisted. So there was no getting out of taking the guitar along for the miserable ride.

With the help of a stranger, I struggle to pull my bags off the moving belt, and The Rat returns with my guitar in his hands, pumping it over his head like it's a trophy.

"It's like a crazy exciting time now," he says. "Sam is really back. Really ready to start Suck again. And this time I think it's going to take!"

We push the bags over to his beat-up hatchback. It sports stickers on the bumper: DESTROY ALL MUSIC and KILL RADIO and KXLU and SEA LEVEL RECORDS and KCRW and AMOEBA RECORDS and INDIE 103, and we have a hard time shoving my bags and the guitar into the backseat because the trunk is filled up with The Rat's drum kit.

"It's not my full drum kit. It's my emergency drum kit," he says. "You know, in case I need to get to some gig or rehearsal last minute."

Normal people keep spare tires and emergency roadside kits in their trunk, but The Rat needs to be able to cover rock emergencies.

I nearly have a heart attack when the car starts because the radio comes on at about one bagazillion decibels. The Rat must have serious ear damage, or, more likely, severe brain damage.

"Let me turn down the music, so we can talk," he says, leaning over. "First of all, I think you should call me Beau, because *The Rat* doesn't sound right for us and *Dad* feels kind of weird. Unless you want to call me Dad? Or The Rat? Or you know what? How about I'll leave it up to you? What do you think?"

As he talks a mile a minute, his hands never stop thumping out a beat on the steering wheel. I don't get a word in edgewise because he just keeps talking and talking and talking, mostly about Suck and their new plans and the old days. Every so often he remembers that I'm in the car and remembers he's excited that I'm here visiting.

I'll just pretend the next two and a half weeks are already over. I'm glad it's a temporary situation. I'll pretend it's a bad dream. That way I'm already back home, with my friends. Living with my mother. Enjoying the rest of my summer.

I try to forget that I am not in Canada today, and that today is Canada Day, our national holiday, July 1.

"This is great," The Rat says, "because I can show you everything. From now on, when I write, you'll be able to picture it all in your head."

He's still babbling away as we walk up the steps to his apartment.

"And see, we're on Sunset Boulevard, so there's plenty for you to do without having a car, 'cause

Los Angeles is mostly a car town. You need a car here. Not like in Montréal."

He tries to say Mun-tree-ul, like a native, and fails.

The Rat unlocks the door to his apartment, stands in the middle of the living room, and spreads his arms out wide.

"Welcome to your temporary home sweet home!" he says.

And then he smiles big and proud.

I take in the view. Model airplanes hang from the ceiling. Colorful, bawdy rock posters cover the walls. The shelves are stacked with too many CDs, too many vinyl records, too many books, and too many DVDs. A full drum kit is squashed into a closet in the corner of the room with foam and egg cartons covering the inside of the closet door. Junk is piled on the floor, on the coffee table, next to the coffee table, and underneath the coffee table, which sits in front of the shabby couch covered by a rag of a knit blanket. I recognize the blanket as one of my mother's knitting projects. Her knitting style is unmistakable. Tiny, complicated patterns—even, perfect, clean. Good yarn. Classy color combinations.

I feel a pang in my chest. I'm already missing her. It's only been one day.

This place is a mess, and it reeks of stale cigarettes poorly masked by room deodorizer. I can't imagine the rest of the apartment looks or smells any better. I want to say, *You could have cleaned up. You knew I was coming.*

But I don't. I don't say a word. I'm polite. I can't help it. The Rat takes off his cowboy hat and throws it on the couch and then rubs his bald head.

"You know, I really meant to straighten up," he says, busily trying to rearrange the mess, like cleaning up now is going to change my first impression. "I just got bogged down with practice. Suck is going to play a secret show on the Fourth of July, and we've been working really hard so we, you know, don't suck. And you know how time just kind of gets away from you? I mean, I kept thinking I had more time, and now suddenly here you are!"

And right there, right that second, my whole heart sinks. Living on the moon with no oxygen would have been easy. Living in a tent in the jungle with no running water and bugs the size of small dogs would have been easy. Living in a cave during the Lower Paleolithic Era, clubbing my own food for dinner while dodging woolly mammoths, would have been easy.

Two and a half weeks of this mess with him, without her, seems impossible.

For some people, clutter is OK. They can live amid chaos, but not me. For me, piles of things on top of things scattered on things equals me not being able to think straight. A mess actually hurts me. Physically.

I know one thing for sure. This is going to be the worst two and a half weeks of my life.

"Excuse me," I say. "I need to go to the bathroom."

"Down the hall," The Rat says.

When I open the door, I think I've made a mistake at first because it doesn't look like a bathroom. It looks like a construction site. There's a ladder leaning against a peeling wall. A bare lightbulb hangs dangerously low from the ceiling. There's a bathtub that once was white but is now caked with yellow lime. The separate shower has a constant drip that I can't turn off, no matter how hard I try. The hand towel has a hole in it. Thankfully, the toilet seems relatively clean. I use the last few squares of toilet paper.

I go to wash my hands. Even the soap is dirty.

I begin to cry.

AMOEBA
ADOLESCENTS

I am still on East Coast time because it is six a.m. according to the clock next to me on the bedside table. I had opened my eyes hoping maybe I'd wake up in a tent in Peru, but no. Bad news. I'm still in L.A.

The first thing I see is that my room is not dingy, which is something I did not notice last night. It has a fresh coat of lavender paint, cheery funky curtains on the windows, and colorful transparent fabrics stapled to the ceiling with rope lights blinking on and off underneath. It looks like The Rat went through a lot of trouble to make my room look cool. But it's for the wrong girl. It's not very *me*. I don't want funky. I want modern. Clean lines. Spare furniture. Neutral colors. Like my room back home.

I turn my face to the window, and from where I lie on the bed, I can see the Hollywood sign. The Hollywood sign is a big disappointment. Surprise! It's totally tiny and boring. They completely misrepresent it in movies. I guess, like most things, it gets too many close-ups so you can't see the whole picture.

It has stopped raining, and the sun streams into the room, forming a yellow square on the painted black wood floor. In that square is a big fat cat sleeping with a paw half over its face like a little drama queen.

The Rat has unpacked my guitar and put it on a guitar stand with a Post-it note on it that says, "All tuned and ready to go!"

Ahhhhh . . . Like I know what do with it. Like I even care. I flick my eyes over to my suitcases in the corner by the door. I know I should unpack, but I won't.

I am not going to stay here in Los Angeles. I cannot stay here. I cannot live with The Rat. Not even for just over two weeks. Not even for one day. I am going to go to Peru and stay with my mother as she scours the Andes for Incan treasures.

I sit on the edge of the bed. In my head, I get up and I grab my bags and go down to the corner very quietly. Can you hail a cab from the street in Los Angeles, like in Montréal? Or do you have to call one, like when I visit Grand-maman at the old age home? I don't care. Somehow, I hail a cab. I use the fifty U.S. dollars that Grand-maman slipped me. It's totally enough. I arrive at the airport and I use the emergency credit card and I buy a ticket non-stop to Lima. In my mind, I do it. In my mind, my feet are moving. In my mind, I am that kind of girl.

The cat meows.

I'm gripping the edge of the bed.

I pick my phone up and text-message my mom. She says I can send text messages anywhere in the world. Even Peru. If I'm going to leave, I'm going to have to do it the right way.

> Mom. Rat is tres drole. Feng shui wrong in
> L.A. Pls wire $ 4 tkt 2 Peru. Luv kd

Hunger forces me to go and explore, so I find the kitchen. The big fat cat, whose name is Sid

Vicious according to its collar, follows me, nipping at my feet, hoping for food. He keeps purring and rubbing up against me. He doesn't live up to his name at all. He's a total softy.

"Don't get too attached to me, Big Guy. I know I'm lovable, but I'm not staying," I say.

I find a basket of fruit hanging over the sink, and after sifting through it, I find one banana that doesn't look too bruised. At least by eating a banana, I don't have to touch any of the dishes, which all seem to be dirty anyway and piled up in the sink. I see something brown and fuzzy floating in one of the cups, and I gag. I can't sit at the table, because there's a half-done model airplane kit spread out on it. I can't sit in this kitchen. It's making me freak out. I open the sliding door that leads onto a tiny balcony and notice that it looks onto a courtyard where a perfectly turquoise-blue swimming pool stares up at me.

Where is the beach? Isn't Los Angeles supposed to be some kind of paradise? Does every single place in Los Angeles have a pool? That's what I saw from the airplane. Tiny blue pools everywhere. Why would you swim in a pool where there is a beach not that far away?

I start daydreaming. I'm swimming in Peru, maybe at a water hole, with a waterfall. Or in a river, with fish nibbling at my toes. Wherever the water would be, I am having the time of my life. Who knows what could happen in Peru? I might even skinny-dip. I might just be that daring. I take swim breaks after assisting Mom on her dig. I'm a real help to Mom on the excavation. She tells me how she just can't do her PhD thesis without me. It really is a godsend that I ran away to Peru. She's not mad at all. She's happy about it. After all, we're a team.

A splash shakes me back to the reality of The Rat's stinky apartment.

A boy is in the pool swimming, doing laps. After a few turns of the length, he changes strokes. I watch him for another five minutes, until he stops and pulls himself out. From here, he looks older than me. From here, he looks like a model. He's wearing a Speedo and I can see everything, even from up here on the balcony.

Sid Vicious, who is sitting with me on the balcony, meows. The boy looks up at me.

You are beautiful, I think. *Let's get lost. Let's run away from this place.* I throw my leg over the balcony and I climb down the grate. I go right up to him. I say, *Hello. My name is Katy and I am your destiny.*

Only not really. Instead I look away, worried that the boy caught me staring, hoping he can't tell all the way from down there that I think he's cute, like somehow he can read my mind. I know he can't. My wild thoughts are mine, safe inside of me.

I hope he lives here. I want to ask The Rat but I can't because he doesn't get out of bed until eleven a.m. I hear his movement in the kitchen and the distinct sound of the coffee grinder grinding beans.

I enter and The Rat is standing there in a pair of worn-thin boxers.

Don't you own a robe? Don't you remember there is a daughter in the house now?

I clear my throat, politely.

The Rat turns and looks at me like he doesn't remember who I am and what the hell I'm doing in his dirty kitchen, then his face turns as red as one of the poppies he has tattooed on his left arm.

"Make coffee." He points. "I'll put my pants on."

He pads out of the room as I take care of the coffee. I am used to the procedure. It makes me comfortable. I always make the coffee for Mom. It's calming. For a quick moment, pouring the water and measuring the grounds feels like home.

As Mom always says, *Plus ça change, plus c'est la même chose.* The more things change, the more they stay the same.

But it was just for a moment. I know full well I am *not* home.

After The Rat has had four cups of strong coffee, he seems ready to talk.

"So," he says. "What should we do?"

"I dunno," I say.

There is nothing I want to do in Los Angeles. Not one thing. Except leave. I'm ready to go. I'm still packed. Just drive me to the airport.

"I cleared my schedule so we could spend a little one-on-one time," he says, dragging on a cigarette. "No band practice. No rock shows. Nada. Just me and you all weekend."

He exhales the smoke in my direction. I cough. He doesn't get the hint.

"Those are bad for you, you know."

I'm just saying. In Canada the cigarette packs are emblazoned with pictures of blackened hearts and lungs. Rotten gums. Tiny deformed babies. It shows you how smoking makes you disgusting. The Rat is disgusting.

"Well, I quit the big things, Katy," he says.

He's talking about Heroin and Alcohol. Those are the big things. His big bad habits, the thing he and Mom had in common. Who started first? I wonder who got who hooked? I only know who quit first.

Mom, because she had a reason.

Me.

"I figure I'll keep the caffeine and the nicotine," The Rat says. "A man's got to have *some* vices."

That makes no sense. I want to ask why. And isn't living in squalor vice enough? Never mind. I won't be here long enough for it to be a problem. It's his funeral. I won't be here long enough to care.

"I'll smoke on the balcony while you're here," The Rat says. "How about that?"

I'm confused. Do I have to answer? That action just seems logical to me. Smoke outside.

"Will you excuse me?" I say. "I think I'll go check my e-mail."

"When you're done, let's have breakfast."

"I already ate," I say, even though all I had was a banana.

"Well, I didn't," The Rat says. "And I'm starving. If you want, I could whip something up here. But usually I go out for breakfast."

I get it. I bet he doesn't cook. I bet he just uses the microwave and heats up chicken potpies. I'm sure that The Rat's idea of cooking is gross bachelor frozen dinners or a can of soup, which is not my style. Mom is a good cook. She even made my baby food herself, and we always eat organic everything.

Tabernac! I am going to starve here in Los Angeles. I just know it. I'll have scurvy or rickets by the end of my visit.

"Just so you know, Mom and I eat only organic," I say, and I shrug. "I don't really eat canned food."

"Neither do I," says The Rat.

Well, what's all this? I want to say. I imagine that I get up and I open the pantry door and dis-

23

play the evidence like I'm on a game show, showing him the shelf of canned food.

"I didn't know what you like to eat so I didn't buy anything," he says. "Other than my earthquake kit, the cupboards are looking pretty Mother Hubbard. We can go to the Farmers Market and get some produce. I have a grill out on the balcony. Do you like grilled food? I love grilled asparagus, even if it makes my pee smell funny. Why *is* that?"

I have to speak quickly or I'm afraid he'll go on about his pee, and I don't want to encourage him.

"Mom makes roasts," I say. "I like roasts."

"It's too hot to roast. We'll find something. That's what cookbooks are for," The Rat says.

Then he opens a cupboard that is too high for me to reach, and displays the long row of cookbooks. I don't care if he has a certificate from a fancy gourmet cooking school. There is no way I would trust the cooking of someone who keeps such a dirty kitchen. I know about salmonella, and I'm not planning on getting it while in Los Angeles.

"I have every intention of being the kind of a person that cooks a lot, but to be honest, I've barely ever cracked any of these books open," The

Rat says. "It's too hard to cook for one. But now that you're here, maybe I'll be inspired. Mostly I just go out to eat, or I order in."

The Rat turns to the counter and pours himself another cup of coffee. Then he turns on the faucet and starts filling up the sink. I hope that he's planning on doing the dishes.

I don't want to help. I retreat to my room.

There are no messages from anyone, not even my best friend, Leticia.

I already miss Montréal, but it doesn't miss me yet.

I decide to e-mail her.

Let . . .
L.A. SUCKS. The Rat's cupboards are filled with canned food. I guess the only thing that's good is that if there is an earthquake, we won't starve, eh? He also smells because of the smoking. What's going on in Montreal? Let me know.
Bisous, Katy

I don't send it. I delete it. I don't want her to think I'm already not having a good time.

REBEL WALTZ
THE CLASH

I'm not surprised when the Fourth of July starts early—on July third. We're in the car by ten a.m., which I've discovered is like the crack of dawn for The Rat, and he informs me that we have two barbecues to hit. I am watching the police helicopters circle lazily above us.

"Is that normal?" I ask. "Is everything all right?"

"What do you mean?" The Rat asks.

"The helicopters," I say.

"Oh, there are always helicopters in Los Angeles—don't sweat it." The Rat laughs. "Unless they are chasing you, which is no fun. I can attest to that."

I don't know that story. The story of The Rat and the police helicopter. I don't want to.

"Blue balloons," he says. "The dealer had the drugs in his mouth in dirty blue balloons."

I want to zone out as he tells me, haltingly, about a time that he bought heroin and was almost busted, running down alleys. He got away. But that wasn't when he hit rock bottom, he says. No. He kept using.

It surprises me that he talks about it so openly, unlike Mom.

I don't want to listen. It feels impolite. Like listening to someone tell you an embarrassing secret. Or like they are wearing their underwear on the outside of their clothes.

It makes me as uncomfortable as the letter I got from him four years ago. It was ten pages long, and rambling. It was too much information, like he felt as though in order to make his apology to me genuine and sincere, he had to tell me every thought he was having in his head. I could barely read it. I got the point. He was sorry.

I stare out the window and watch the cars, and the bright of the day, and the blue sky, and the neighborhoods, and I can't help noticing how everything here is so spread out, the landscape changing from strip malls to houses to clusters of low-rent stores. It doesn't feel like a city to me. It doesn't feel like Los Angeles has a center.

"I'm playing in three bands at the Punk House. It's a tradition," he says. "But I have to stop at this other BBQ first. You know, put in an appearance."

"Fireworks are a tradition, too," I say. But he doesn't seem to hear me; he just goes on with telling me the plan. He is always talking. Clearly The Rat can't stand silence. I wish he'd just be quiet.

I like quiet.

"First there's the party at the Yellow House. We'll just stop in there for a quick hello. A bunch of guys on their day off from the Warped Tour will be there, and I want to let them know that Suck is playing, that we're back together. Then we'll jet over to the Punk House for the all-day Fourth of July Jam."

"I thought you were taking time off for me," I say.

"Well, I am. The first two aren't my real bands, and then Suck is playing a secret show."

Playing in three shows in three different bands in one day doesn't count as playing too much to The Rat.

I want to wave out the window at one of the helicopters up in the sky. *Take me away*, I think. *Come get me out of here! Rescue me! Send down a ladder! Shut him up! I'm being talked to death! I don't want to hear one more thing about Suck.*

But the helicopter passes us by, in pursuit of lesser crimes.

"I can't believe how good the timing is that you'll get to see Suck's first show in years. Is that kismet or what?"

"I want to see fireworks," I say. But I don't really.

"Well, someone's bound to have some that they'll shoot off, though it's probably not going to be some big spectacular show. OK?"

"It'll have to do," I say, sighing. Besides, nothing would beat the International Fireworks Festival Competition they have in Montréal. I wish I were there.

The Rat gets a funny look in his eyes.

"What?" I ask.

"We had a picnic at this fireworks thing in Montréal. Me, you, and your mom. I went with you guys once. The sound scared you, so you stuck your head under my shirt the whole night."

"I don't remember that." I really don't. I'm not lying.

"Oh, yeah. You were like two years old," The Rat says, kind of trying to hide the disappointment in his voice. "It was the first time I came to Montréal, so I could meet you."

You were never there. Mom and I go to the fireworks every year. Me and Mom. Me and Mom are a team. A team you are not on.

We're quiet for a while. I am trying to remember all the times I have hung out with The Rat, and they don't amount to much. Just a bunch of lunches at St-Hubert Chicken, a few trips to the Insectarium, some kiddie movies. It was all when I was really little, and Mom would never be there when he would pick me up. He'd come to Grand-maman's house, and she wouldn't let him in. He'd have to wait for me in the hall.

And then, when I was seven, he stopped coming.

"Is he ever going to come back?" I finally asked. I didn't really care. He wasn't that big a deal. I hardly knew him. But I was curious.

"No," Mom said.

"Don't you care?" I asked.

"Yes," she said.

"But you don't want to see him again."

"No. But I'm sad for you, Katy."

"Why isn't he coming?"

"He tried to bring drugs into Canada, and they caught him and they told him he could never come back," Mom said.

"Never?"

"Never."

"That's a long time," I said.

"Yes, never is a long time."

"Why would he do that?" I asked. "Why would he try to bring drugs here?"

"Because he's an addict," Mom said. "Just like me."

"But you don't do drugs," I said.

"No. I don't. Not anymore. But I still have the disease."

And that is the deepest she ever went into it with me. She changes the subject whenever the word *drugs* or *addiction* comes up. She makes some tea. Or bakes a cake. Or goes to her room and calls Grand-maman. She has to talk to someone about it. It's just not to me.

So I stopped bringing it up.

The Rat didn't really mean that much to me anyway.

After his big long apology letter, he never really mentioned not being able to come into Canada to see me. Not once in all the postcards sent from the road and stuff. He'd just say that he was on "adventure time." That road trips were fun. That he wished I could see rock tours the way he sees them. He never mentioned that I never really wrote him back. Maybe it makes him uncomfortable, too.

The Rat starts tapping away on the steering wheel. He goes back to his favorite subject. Suck.

I'm beginning to see how this works. When in doubt, bring up Suck. Awkward silence? Talk about Suck.

"You'll get to meet Sam Suck, my best friend. We've known each other since junior high school."

Hidden in my mom's bedroom, inside a shoe-box in the back of her closet, there's a photo of her, The Rat, and Sam Suck. Whenever I am curious about The Rat, I go to the shoebox and dig through it. I examine the trinkets from my mom's past. There's that picture. There's a leather choker with a fleur-de-lys on it. A plastic ring, the kind that looks like it came out of a gumball machine. A bunch of lanyards for rock shows, and various VIP backstage passes. Bad Religion. Black Flag. Circle Jerks. Red Hot Chili Peppers. Thelonious Monster. Nirvana. D.I. Social Distortion. Sonic Youth. fIREHOSE. Jane's Addiction. A beer cap with a hole in it. A *Flipside* magazine with Suck on the cover. A book of matches from someplace called Al's Bar. Another book from a place called Jabberjaw, with *BR + LB* written in a heart on the inside. A sketch of The Rat and my mom, ripped out of a notebook, with *10/27 outside of Raji's* scrawled at the bottom. A broken drumstick. A bandana. A scrap of paper with curly writing on it. *Let's be friends! Yana Banana* and a phone number.

They are artifacts of my mother's time with The Rat. I want to understand why these keepsakes are important. I want to piece together the story.

"I'm not *that girl* anymore," Mom always says when I ask her.

They are the only things I've ever seen from that time before I was born, before she left behind that alternative lifestyle and never spoke of it again. Before she became my mom.

"It's like those Greek myths," she says, "where someone has to go to Hades and back to get the one that they love. I went to Hell and back and I found you."

In the photo, Mom has long blond dreadlocks and she's standing between The Rat and Sam Suck. The Rat only has a few tattoos on his arms. He's skinny—skin and bones—and he looks really young. They all do. Sam Suck has a tiny Mohawk, which has kind of flopped over on its side, and there is a cigarette hanging out of his mouth. His eyes are half closed. My mom has her arms thrown around their shoulders. They look as though they are holding her up, like she can't stand on her own two feet. Her head is tilted back and she's laughing. Her smile is disarming. She looks totally happy. She looks totally free.

I love that picture for her laugh.

I have never once seen her laugh like that with me.

With me, her laughs have a little twinge of sadness, a little bit of something being held back. Or so it seems. Like she had to leave her real laugh behind in Hell. Like that laugh belongs to *that girl*. In that picture, I imagine that her laugh comes right from her belly.

I have never laughed like that either.

I just know I haven't. I always hold something back, too.

All I know is that I come from Hell. And The Rat and Sam Suck are where Hell begins. And now I'm with them.

In Hell.

HOLIDAY IN CAMBODIA

DEAD KENNEDYS

The Yellow House is a nice house filled with nice normal people. They look like they have money. Even though there are some dreadlocks and spiked hair in the crowd, everyone looks clean-cut. There are a lot of kids running around, but not one of them is my age. It's all babies and toddlers.

"Why are there so many babies here?" I ask.

"They all started breeding late," The Rat says.

He probably means they didn't knock up a teenage girl like he did when he was twenty-seven.

The Rat grabs a soda pop and then I follow him as he goes over to a bunch of guys, all wearing black jeans, colorful button-down shirts, and black-rimmed glasses.

After he introduces me to everyone, he gives me a little eyebrow lift, which I think is supposed to signal that these guys he's standing with, who wave and nod at me, whoever they are, are really cool, and that they make him really cool.

Maybe I've seen them on *Much Music* in a video that I ignored because they are old guys and not the kind of boys that Leticia and I find cute. I don't mind bands that have cute boys in them, but these old guys are like in their *forties*.

But I have to admit that even though they are not my style, they sure do look cooler than The Rat. Even just standing around these guys look like they could be on the cover of a magazine. They all have this ease about them, a kind of calm as they stand around eating. Not like The Rat. The Rat always has that jumpy nervous energy, drumming a beat out on anything he can tap his hands on, that makes me feel a little panicked.

I keep my gaze steady. I smile instead of rolling my eyes. I remain neutral. I nod enthusiastically, feigning interest as The Rat tells me that his friends are all in really big bands. But I don't know who the guys are, and even though some of them look vaguely familiar, I'm unimpressed.

The Rat and the cool-looking crowd gather to one spot by the grill as one of the guys occupies himself by flipping the meat. They immediately get into an intense discussion. Then I think The Rat forgets I'm there with him. He's probably not used to having someone tag along. He's probably used to being a loner.

I don't care. I zone out and just watch them talk. It's as intense as the academic discussions between Mom and her colleagues, only The Rat and these guys are no intellectuals. They are not trying to solve existential questions. They are not debating the meaning of life, or the origins of the universe.

They are talking about golf.

"Well, my slice was back in full force, so I couldn't get a par to save my life," someone says.

"Why don't you just admit that you suck?"

They laugh.

"I just got this new sixty-degree wedge that I think should finally help my short game."

"Have you played the Beverly Hills course?"

"No. We should go there."

"I'm a member of that club, so I can get us a tee time."

"Great, next Thursday."

"I'm in," The Rat says.

"Me, too," someone else chimes in.

Unbelievable. The Rat plays golf? I try to picture it, but I just can't.

"Rat," I say. "Rat."

"Oh, hey. Katy." Like he's suddenly remembering that I'm there. Clearly I should be wearing a T-shirt that says I'M WITH CLUELESS.

"See, your Pops doesn't just play drums well," one of the guys says. "He plays a mean game of golf, too."

Everyone laughs.

It's not that funny. Or, maybe the conversation is funny for aging punk rock people, but not for me. It's boring. I can't even follow the conversations they are having around me. I have no *in*. No common ground. There is no thread for me to hang on to, which makes me zone out. Instead, I make up conversations I'd be having with Leticia if she were here with me. We'd maybe talk about their clothes. Leticia is really into clothes.

I think they look normal*ish*. Their jeans look

expensive. Their shirts are pressed. Their shorts are stylish. And their sneakers are hip. Next to them, The Rat just looks like Pigpen. He looks wrinkled and faded and threadbare. They look money, and he looks poor.

"Man, what I wouldn't give for one of your careers," The Rat says.

Everybody laughs. Even The Rat is trying to pass it off as funny now, though it's obvious he was being truthful.

"But Suck is legendary," one of the guys says.

"Well, 'legendary' didn't buy me a house," The Rat says. "I'm still stuck in the Rat Hole at Grunge Estates."

"Aw, Rat. We just had better bands," one of them says jokingly.

"Bigger hits."

"Better luck."

"Sober sooner," The Rat adds.

They all laugh again. They laugh easily. Move easily. I notice that out of the six of them, only two are drinking beer.

"We'd better go," The Rat says. "See you guys at the Punk House."

"Yeah," one of them says. "I can't wait to see

Suck live again. You guys always put on the best shows."

"Yeah, we destroyed," The Rat says. "Literally."

The Punk House looks relatively tame from the outside, but as I help carry The Rat's drum kit inside, I almost throw up. The inside of the house is even worse than the Rat Hole.

The carpet is stained. Crusted, even—possibly with puke. There are bottles and cans and overflowing ashtrays everywhere. The pizza boxes on the table in the dining area are swarming with ants. The kitchen sink is filled with unwashed dishes. I don't know where to look. So I look up.

There is mold on the ceiling.

"Oh my God. This is disgusting," I say. I can't help it. It's too awful to keep to myself.

"Beware," The Rat says. "Punk rock bachelors live here."

"That's what you are," I say.

"I was never this bad." He laughs. "Besides, you don't need a penicillin shot after you go to the bathroom at my house."

"I hope you're kidding," I say. I don't want to have to hold my bladder all day.

"Of course I'm kidding," The Rat says.

"I don't even know where to put my feet," I say. "I might break something. Or catch something."

"Screw it. Step on anything," The Rat says.

The Rat just walks over stuff, but I still can't help it; I try to watch where my feet are going.

We exit with the drum kit to the huge back-yard. On a makeshift stage, there is an all-girl band playing surf music. The freaky slides and sounds complement the visual assault I'm experiencing. American flags hang everywhere, but the colors people wear are not confined to a patriotic red, white, and blue, and the colors are not just on their clothes. Everyone's hair is dyed in a rainbow of shades, and they all have tattoos, tattoos, TAT-TOOS! I suspect that The Rat is the oldest person here because they all look like teenagers, but when I get a closer look, I realize that almost everyone here is old. Everyone got older but forgot to grow up.

The scene is completely surreal, like a Dali painting or something. I imagine this is what trip-ping feels like.

I'm not freaked out by the amount of inked

skin or the colors in people's hair or the clothes that they wear. Montréal is one of the most tattooed cities in North America. I just haven't seen so many people like The Rat all crowded together into one place. I've never been surrounded by so many people not like me.

I'm the odd girl out.

The Rat just kind of leaves me to my own devices as he checks in with people and says his hellos. I don't see how I can fit in here. I *can't* fit in here. I make my escape and find myself blissfully alone by the guacamole. But not for long.

"So, you're Katy," one guy says, rounding up a plate of chips at the other end of the table. "I'm Sam."

For a punk rock legend, he's quiet. Uncrazy. Unlike the guy in the Mohawk in the photo that I know by heart. Unlike the Suck poster I saw at The Rat's house, where he is scary sweat and blood and holding his guitar like a weapon. Unlike the screaming face on that reissued CD. Sam Suck has shaggy brown hair peppered with gray that falls long onto his shoulders. His eyes are pale icy blue, one of his teeth is kind of grayish, and the lines on his face are deep, like scars. His eyebrows are bushy and meet in the middle. He doesn't look punk to me. He just looks like just another old guy.

He sticks his hand out. He's the only one who's offered me his hand.

I take it. We shake.

He nods.

"You look like your mom," he says.

I know I don't look anything like my mom. I never have. My skin isn't olive; it's pale. My hair isn't blond and curly; it's flat and dark and useless, the kind that only looks good in a ponytail. I got my hair from The Rat, even though now he shaves his head because he's going bald. I have a plain face. Normal. Uninteresting. Average. Unremarkable. My mom's features are startling. They are wide and almost too large for her face. Her ears stick out. Her nose is bent. Her teeth are crooked. Even with her mainstream look she can never hide her unusual features, so I know he is lying when he says I look like her.

The way he looks at me makes me want to be honest. His ice-blue eyes don't take any bullshit.

So I speak. I say it. I call him on it. I tell him what's what.

"I don't look like my mom at all."

"You do," he says. "It's those eyes. Different color. Same eyes."

No one has ever said that to me before. My mom may have goofy features, but she has the kind of eyes that you want focused on you because they really seem to see things.

I want her eyes on me now. I want her looking at me now, not Sam Suck.

"How's she doing?" he asks, smoothing out the potentially awkward moment.

"She's in Peru, studying the Incas." I won't choke up in front of a stranger. I won't.

"She cleaned up good," Sam says. He nods in approval.

"I see you've met Sam," The Rat says, joining us with a beer in one hand and a plate of food in the other. I'm actually kind of hungry and glad that The Rat has brought me a burger. I am about to reach for the plate when he sets down his beer and takes a bite of the burger. I see. It's *his* plate. He didn't get me anything to eat at all.

"I thought you didn't drink," I say.

"Nothing like a near-beer on a hot summer day," he says.

The Rat and Sam laugh, like it's a private joke. They clink near-beer bottles.

A girl with stringy thin dyed-black hair, black jeans, and a black T-shirt that says BUST on it comes up to Sam. She hands him a bunch of colorful little plastic triangles.

"Dad, here are your picks," she says.

I have to bite the inside of my cheeks to keep from laughing. Her voice is impossibly high, like a cartoon, like she's been sucking on helium or like there is not enough room in her throat. I almost think her voice is a joke, except for the dirty look she gives me, which tells me she gets that reaction all the time.

"Lake, this is Katy, Rat's kid. She's staying here for a couple of weeks," Sam says.

"Fourteen more days. Then I go home to Montréal," I say. Just to be clear that I'm not sticking around.

Lake looks me over. I can tell she doesn't approve of my khaki shorts and pale pink T-shirt. I know I don't fit in. She doesn't have to remind me.

"Hi," she says.

Then The Rat and Sam Suck exchange knowing looks. Lake rolls her eyes like we're all stupid.

I know what's coming. We're going to be forced on each other. I don't want to have to be The Rat's sidekick all day. Lake will have to do.

"Lake," The Rat says. "Remember our agreement?"

She sighs.

"Come on," Lake says in her squeaky voice. She jerks her head toward the party, indicating for me to follow. I do. I'd rather go than stay.

"Have fun, Katy," The Rat says. "But not too much fun. You know, be cool, but not too cool."

Could I *be* more humiliated?

I have to walk fast to keep up with Lake because she's already split. Mom says when you're in a new environment, ask questions. So I do. I ask. But getting answers from Lake is like pulling teeth.

"How old are you?"

"Sixteen," she says.

"What grade are you in?" I ask.

"Junior."

"Oh, I'm going to be in Secondary Four," I say.

"What?"

"Secondary Four," I say. "It's like grade ten in American high school."

"*Listen,*" she says, tugging on her ear.

"To what?" I ask.

She rolls her eyes and gestures toward the band taking the stage.

"No talking while there is rocking," she says.

Here we go again. The band starts and it is too loud. I put my fingers in my ears.

"I think you are right: *ils sont trop* loud to talk," I say, yelling Franglais above the music.

Lake laughs at me, almost doing a spit take with her soda.

"You speak French? Won't do you any good here. You gotta learn to *habla español.*"

We stop talking because at this point the music gets out of control and no one can talk. I try covering my ears even more as the volume seems to go from a level eight to a level twelve. After a few minutes, Lake taps me on the shoulder and hands me a little plastic package with two foamy pieces inside.

"Here," she yells. "Don't leave home without them."

"What are they?" I ask.

"Ear condoms," Lake says.

I open up the package and shove the little foamy plugs in my ears. Looking around, I notice that everyone has them stuck in their ears and that there are bowls of earplugs and real condoms scattered around the party. The little signs above the bowls say: BE SAFE! PLAY SAFE! ROCK SAFE!

When the band stops playing, everyone hoots and hollers.

Lake points to my ears, and I pull the earplugs out.

"So what's your deal?" she says. Is she just making conversation until the next band takes the stage? Or is she really interested in me?

I shrug. My ears are still ringing. I bet I get tinnitus.

In my head, I tell her I have a lot of friends in Montréal and she doesn't have to babysit me. I don't mind being alone for two more weeks. I *like* being alone. In my head, I tell her I am technically going to be a year behind her, but the education system is better in Canada than in the United States, so I'm probably more advanced than she is. I tell her that I walk everywhere in Montréal. And I like it. I tell her she smells like BO. I tell her that I think I see lice in her hair.

But in reality, I keep my mouth shut. I shrug for a second time. I put the earplugs back in my ears. It drowns out the *babble babble babble* of the party.

Lake doesn't care. I can tell by the way her body is turned away from me. The time for talking is now over. A new band has taken the stage. She is at complete attention. She is transfixed by the music. She is devouring the stage with her eyes. It's not like we're together; it's more like we're just standing next to each other. It's merely out of convenience or proximity.

She's clapping. I can't believe she actually wants to be here. She wants to mingle with these kinds of adultescents. She wants to be listening to this stuff, this *noise*. It's not anything I have ever heard on the radio. It's not easy to listen to. It's scary. I like music to be in the background. Not in my face.

I do not want to be here. I don't bother looking around for The Rat, because I don't want to be with him either. I just can't wait for this day to be over. I pretend the noise and the crazy adults and the stupid American barbecue food aren't here. I pretend I'm not here.

I am far away. I am back home. I am in Montréal. I am at the *piscine*. I am eating *poutine*. I am at the *dépanneur* with Leticia buying an ice-cream sandwich. We're going to go hang out at Parc Lafontaine.

But I can't focus on it. I can't. I can't conjure up the image to teleport me there. It's too loud. Everything here is too loud. Even with the earplugs.

I try to zone out again, between bands. I float away in the pocket of silence until I am shaken out of my reverie by a sonic boom. At least that's what I think it is. I let out a yelp.

Lake laughs at me again.

"Relax," Lake says. "It's just feedback from one of the amps."

She likes that I don't know anything. Thinking I'm stupid probably makes her feel good about herself. She climbs up on a plastic chair so that she can see better. She puts her fingers in her mouth and whistles like a trucker.

Suck is the band now taking the stage. Everyone at the party starts to stumble closer. They all want to see. Mob mentality makes me want to see, too. I climb up on a chair next to Lake.

The Rat takes his place and sits behind his drum kit, shirtless. Sam quietly stands at the microphone as the entire party becomes still. He just stands there with intention. I lean forward. I almost tip off the chair. No one dares to breathe.

Suddenly, The Rat breaks the spell, clicking the drumsticks over his head. He screams, "ONE, TWO, THREE, FOUR!"

And then he crashes his sticks on the drums. Smashes them. They explode. Like they are bombs. Sam Suck is no longer the quiet gentleman that I met by the guacamole. He is screaming. He is all noise and insanity. He is all jumping and falling and throwing and attacking the air with his body. He is all danger and pain.

I've got a knot in my stomach.

I don't know what's going to happen.

I'm afraid.

The people in front of the makeshift stage are dancing wildly. Their bodies smash into each other. They push and claw. They use each other to gain energy and force. The music is coaxing the crazy out of them. I don't like it.

Now I shrink back from the noise. I can't even look at The Rat. He has an evil look on his face. An evil grin. This is not the same person that picked me up from the airport. This is a real rat. A no-good carrier of the plague. Only The Rat's plague is *music*. Angry, angry music. Pounding on those drums. Punishing those skins. Torturing us all.

This sounds nothing like the album I heard at home. It's worse.

Sam Suck grabs at the microphone. He attacks it with his words.

> *"When I stand at attention*
> *I'm really asking questions*
> *Like what the hell is up with you?*
> *Your red?*
> *Your white?*
> *Your fucking blue?*
> *And when I go to cast my vote*
> *I'm unimpressed with your one note,*
> *People spitting back what you quote.*
> *I won't learn your words by rote."*

By the end of the set, The Rat is sweaty. No. *Sweaty* is too polite a word. He's a pig. He's a sweaty pig, dripping rivers from his body as he gets up and throws his sticks into the audience. And Sam Suck's knuckles are bleeding; his hair is soaking wet and sticking to his face grotesquely, like long tentacles or snakes. The Rat pushes over his drum kit and it falls into a heap on the ground. Then he tackles Sam Suck. They roll around on the stage, laughing and groping each other, fake fighting, fake fucking. Everyone else is laughing and goading them on.

Sam Suck gets up off the floor. He spits on the side of the stage. He picks up the microphone.

Then he speaks.

"My name is Sam Suck. And I have something to say. I stand for all that is true. I vow to be myself at all times. Speak out when I can. Not be afraid of the repercussions of having a voice that might not be in accordance with the mainstream. I vow to think for myself. I vow to make sure that I am always asking questions. I will go my own way. I am unique. And I swear you are, too. So stand up and be heard. Stand up unafraid. We're going to think out, speak out, act out for social change. Do not be afraid to declare yourself a punk. Everyone who is a thinking, feeling, questioning person who stands up for truth is a punk. I salute you."

Then he flips everyone his middle finger with one hand and pushes over the microphone with the other, and the crowd goes wild. They are pumping their fists in the air. They start screaming. Like a chant. Like an anthem.

"FUCK YOU!"

"FUCK YOU!"

"FUCK YOU!"

They yell beside me and around me while I shrink to the smallest size I ever was. Small like a child. Like a frightened mouse.

"They're something else, huh?" Lake says in her baby voice—no change in her. She's all cool and clapping, sometimes throwing a fist in the air. Devil's horns. Or middle finger. Or truck-stop whistling.

I don't even know what to say.

I may have swallowed my own tongue.

She sees my fear—I can tell. And she disapproves. She rolls her eyes.

"God, you're so *beige*," she says.

*   *   *

I fake being asleep in the car all the way home, so when The Rat asks me how I liked the show, I just kind of mumble incoherently. I must do a pretty good job of faking, because he just leaves me be and drives while beating out a peppy beat on the steering wheel. That suits me just fine. I am glad. I don't have any good answers for the kinds of questions he might ask me.

I don't even think what Suck plays *is* music. And that "concert" was not like any concert I ever went to. Once I went with Leticia to see Boy Bomb. We had assigned seats and it was in a theater. And the boys on stage had dance moves that were coordinated. That's the kind of music I can swallow. It was all very civilized. I even bought a program and a T-shirt.

When we get home, I just excuse myself, go to my room, and close the door. I write Mom an e-mail. She might not even get it, but it makes me feel better to send it.

Mom,
The Rat's friends behave like juvenile delinquents. I'm sure that child welfare services

are going to take me away. Also, Suck
sucks. I'm sure that I've already suffered
permanent hearing loss from the noise they
call music. Better send that ticket to Lima
before I have to learn sign language.
Bisous, Katy.

I send it out into the ether. Like a cyber message in a bottle. SOS.

CALIFORNIA ÜBER ALLES

DEAD KENNEDYS

The Rat is so into showing me the city of Los Angeles. He's making all sorts of efforts.

"It gets a bad rap, but this city is great," he says.

It's officially true that you can only stand seeing so much touristy stuff before your head explodes. It's also officially true that The Rat and I won't agree on what constitutes a "cool tourist thing to do," which is why we are sitting at the Hamburger Hamlet not talking to each other while he eats a California burger and I eat a veggie burger.

I now know the entire sordid history of Suck. I know everything about Suck. I could get a PhD in Suck.

I look out the window while The Rat starts talking. There are a bunch of people taking pictures of the feet in the cement (BORING) and taking pictures with people who are dressed up like Charlie Chaplin and Marilyn Monroe and various other pop culture demons (WEIRDOS).

I point across the street to Mann's Chinese Theater.

"Does somebody pay those people?" I ask.

"What?" The Rat says.

"Those people dressed up as celebrities. Does somebody pay them to do that? Is that their job?"

"I don't think they're paid. Charlie Chaplin asked me for a dollar once," The Rat says. "I took my picture with her. It's a woman. I tried to leave and she grabbed me with her arm, strong grip, and she whispered through her fake smile, 'Give me a dollar.'"

"It's kind of a weird job," I say.

"Oh, I have had weirder." He kind of eases his shoulders now that we are talking and not being quiet. I think the quiet drives him crazy. But I think he's trying to be quiet for me.

"Like what?"

"Costumed message-delivery boy and singing telegram dressed as a gorilla usually. Making balloon animals at kiddie parties," he says. "Oh! And a member of the midnight flamingo assault squad."

"What's that?"

"For a fee, we would sneak onto people's lawns and plant hundreds of pink plastic flamingos."

"Mom's been a receptionist, a salesgirl, a waitress, and a research assistant."

"That's a far cry from the Leda I knew," The Rat says.

I know her best. *I* do.

"She likes research assistant and teacher's assistant best," I say.

"Your mom was a squeegee punk when I met her."

My mom? A squeegee punk? One of those dirty kids who wash your windows uninvited at red lights? They are disgusting. She's never told me that she used to be one of them. That she could relate to their begging for change. She never told me to be quiet when I spoke about how disgusting · they were. Now I understand why

Mom always rolls down her window and gives them loonies.

"It's just a dollar," she always says.

I don't let The Rat know that I didn't know about that. I just put my burger in my mouth. Like, *Oh, yeah. Squeegee punk. Right. Forgot about that one.*

"Did you kidnap her?" I ask finally. "Grandmaman always says you kidnapped her."

It's one of those unanswered questions that no one ever answers around me.

The Rat does a drumroll on the table.

I hold my breath. This is where the story always ends. This is where the subject gets changed. This is where my mystery begins. This is where the questions I always ask remain unanswered.

"No, your mom stowed away on the bus. I found her under the covers of my bunk when we got to Ottawa."

"What happened then?"

"I kissed her."

"Did you like her?"

"No, I didn't even know her name. She was just a groupie on the bus."

"What happened then?"

The Rat takes the saltshaker in his hand and starts to spin it around. His eyes seem to focus on something far away.

"After the show in Ottawa, we all went to an after-hours party. We all got drunk."

"And high?" I ask.

"Maybe."

He starts to look uncomfortable, but I don't want him to stop. Not now. I gesture with my hand for him to go on.

The Rat takes a deep breath. He pats his pocket where he keeps his cigarettes and then glances at the no smoking sign and puts his hand on the table. Starts drumming his fingers.

I remind myself to breathe as he opens his mouth and begins to speak.

"Your mom and I ended up on the roof of this warehouse. She started screaming at the city. Just howling. So, I started howling, too. Then we lay down on the roof, and I thought here was my big chance to have wild sex with this cute, crazy girl. I thought, I'll just roll over and throw it in her."

Ew, gross, I think. But I don't dare say anything that might make him stop telling me the story.

Layers and layers deep. I am diving right to the bottom. At last he's telling me something I'm interested in.

"I turned to her ready to make my move and she looked at me with those wicked green eyes of hers and she opened her mouth and she said something along the lines of 'I want to be able to float away in my body so I can finally catch up with my mind.' And she took my hand and no hand has ever felt like that. So *real*. It was like suddenly I was completely inhabiting my own body, too. All I wanted to do was look into her eyes on that roof and hold her hand and never let it go."

"But you did," I say. "You did let it go."

"Well, that's another story," The Rat says, leaning back in his chair, like he's lighter. Like a weight has been removed from him. "But you should add merch girl to the rest of the jobs that she's had. She sold our merch for the rest of the tour all the way to California. That's how she got here and I'm why she stayed."

"Until she left," I say.

"Yeah, until then."

Because of *me*.

And now I know the real story of how Mom met The Rat. But I notice that he doesn't say how he was twenty-seven and she was sixteen and how she got hooked on heroin and ran away from Los Angeles back to Montréal with a baby in her belly. And how that was *wrong*.

He was *wrong*.

"What's done is done," Mom says. "It just happened that way. I was young. I was stupid. I told him I was eighteen. I thought it was so cool. I've moved on."

"What about you?" I ask The Rat. "What do you do now?"

"Besides rock star?" He laughs. He does a drumroll. "To pay the bills, I'm an art preparator. I've got a toolbox and I know how to use it."

"What's an art preparator?"

"I install art and installations in museums, galleries, and homes. It's flexible and steady and I can go on the road if I need to."

I mull it over while I sip my coffee.

"Why don't you just get a real job?"

The Rat looks like he didn't understand the question.

"What?" I say.

Then he laughs while shaking his head. "The point is, Katy, those were all real jobs."

"Not squeegee punk," I say.

"Yes," he says. "In a way it was."

When we get back to the house, I go to my room and I hear The Rat shuffling around in the living room.

I wrap my special knit blanket around me, savoring the one puzzle piece I have now, one thing that clicks into place. I think about everything, and before long, I fall asleep.

"Do you know what I like best about us?" Mom says.

I do know, but I like it when she tells me. I like to hear her say it.

"I like that we're friends," she says.

"Me, too."

"It took me a long time be friends with my mother," she says.

BLISTER IN THE SUN

VIOLENT FEMMES

The fan in the apartment just moves the hot air around. It's so hot I don't want to eat lunch.

"Don't you have air-conditioning?"

"No. It's only really unbearable in August," The Rat says.

He's sitting on the couch with his drumsticks hitting on a practice pad.

"It's unbearable now," I say.

"At least it's not humid," The Rat says. "God, I hate humid."

"But it's still hot."

Hot as Hell, I think.

"Go take a swim," The Rat says without looking up from his *SPIN* magazine. "Knock yourself out."

I wonder if he really means, *Get out of here—I'm reading.*

I leave my lunch on the table and head to my room to put on my bathing suit. Standing in front of the full-length mirror, I can tell one thing for sure: it's a good thing I'm not staying here for too long, or I'd be an embarrassment.

I'm sure I look West Coast terrible.

I'm paler than pale and I have no boobs to fill the top of my swimsuit. Leticia calls them speed tits.

She calls hers bodacious tatas.

She always rubs it in. She looks like a woman, and I still look like a little girl.

When I go back to the kitchen, The Rat hasn't moved. I open the freezer and get a piece of ice to suck on, then I go to the balcony and check out the pool action. I don't want to go down there if that boy is swimming. I don't want him to see me in my bathing suit. But he's not there. There's only a lady sporting a big orange hat, sunning herself in one of the lounge chairs.

I pop the ice out of my mouth and rub it on the back of my neck and my wrists as I head down to the pool.

The woman looks up at me as I open the gate.

"You must be Beau's girl."

"Yah. Katy."

I start to put my foot in the pool.

"I'm not going to be responsible for you," she says, eyes on her magazine.

"Excuse me?"

"No minors can swim without adult supervision." She points at a sign.

I look to where she's pointed and she's right: tacked onto the gate is a sign that says no minors are allowed to swim without adult supervision.

"Well, what am I supposed to do?"

"Not my problem," the woman says, still not looking up.

I consider going upstairs to get The Rat, but for the first time since I've arrived in Los Angeles, I'm alone, and I want to keep it that way for just a bit longer.

I could disobey the rules. I could just swim anyway. I could be the kind of girl who would break the rules. But I know I'm not. I just sit down on the edge of the pool and slip my legs into the cool water and then lie back onto the cement and look up at the blue cloudless sky.

A silver glint catches my eyes, and I scan the

balconies facing the courtyard. My eyes fall on the swimmer from the other day. He's sitting on his balcony, talking on the phone. I watch him as his mouth forms O's as he speaks. He looks exactly like the kind of boy that you would meet in California. He's tan. He's fit. He's beautiful.

If I could meet him, I could go back home with a real story. He could save me from having a bad time here. Like a knight in shining armor. Maybe he's a TV star. He's that dreamy. I could just say he was. I could brag about it to Leticia. My time in Hollywood hanging out with a famous actor.

"People make the best sunshade, don't you think?" A woman holding a toddler towers over me, effectively blocking the sun. She is wearing a black vintage swimsuit and a straw hat and cat-eye sunglasses. Tattooed around the entire top of her right arm is a ring of fairies afloat on a field of flowers, and on the bicep of her left sits a mermaid. She has an anchor tattooed on her forearm.

"Do you want to swim?" she asks.

"Yeah."

"I'll watch you."

Her baby is blond and bubbly. He reaches for me.

"Mine," he says.

"This is Auggie. I'm Trixie. You must be Katy."

"Yeah," I say, getting up to shake her hand.

She puts down Auggie and opens up her bag, which is covered with a skull-and-crossbones motif, unlike any diaper bag I've ever seen. She pulls out a little life vest and straps it onto him.

"Go ahead. I'll watch. Besides, as long as Leo is up on his balcony, we're all safe," Trixie says.

Leo. The boy's name is Leo.

"He can't dive from up there. He'd hit his head on the bottom of the pool," the woman in the orange hat says, still not looking up from her magazine.

Trixie looks at me and rolls her eyes. I roll my eyes right back. We both smile.

I dive into the pool and let the water slide over me. Trixie hangs out by the steps with Auggie as he splashes the water and squeals with pleasure. Little kids are so easily amused.

After a couple of laps, I swim over to Trixie.

"I'm glad you were out here. I was going to

come over and say hello. Beau had mentioned you were visiting," she says. "I'm his girlfriend."

"Oh." He seems to be so open with everything else, I wonder why he didn't mention a girlfriend. I thought he was a loner. I never heard him ever mention any woman except for my mother. I try to picture him attempting to woo someone. I can't.

I must look surprised, because Trixie shrugs and laughs again. "He's probably still working up the courage to talk to you about it. Men. They are so strange."

"I wouldn't know."

"Don't you have boyfriends?" Trixie asks.

"No."

"What about your mom? She must have boy-friends."

"No," I say.

"Not ever?"

I wonder if she's fishing for information. I want to tell her to mind her own business. I want to tell her to talk to the hand.

"No," I say.

"Hmm," Trixie says. "That's a shame."

No, it's not, I think. My mom doesn't need a man to make her happy. She's happy by herself, with me.

Auggie slaps the water with his hand and squints his little eyes and smiles. Then he reaches for me.

"He likes you!" Trixie says. "I think that means we're going to be great friends."

I look at her. She's not even like a real person. She's like a person who's stepped out of a 1950s movie. I wonder if she dresses like that all the time.

"Anyway, Auggie's a good judge of character. Aren't you, Auggie? Aren't you?" Trixie grabs Auggie's little body and blows a raspberry on his stomach, which sends Auggie right over the moon.

Watching Trixie with Auggie makes me hurt for Mom. I wonder what she's doing today. I wonder if the site is everything she'd hoped. I wonder if she's missing me. I dive back under the water so that even I don't know if my face is just wet or if I'm actually crying.

I pull myself out of the pool and grab my towel and head upstairs. I don't want to hang out here.

"See you," I say, not looking her in the eyes.

"Welcome to Grunge Estates, Katy," she calls after me.

GIRL U WANT

DEVO

Someone is leaning on the unbearably loud buzzer at the door.

"Katy, can you get that?" The Rat says. He's in the bathroom. Taking a long time. Stinking it up. Reading magazines. The Rat poops more than anyone I know.

"Who is it?" I say through the door.

"It's Lake," I hear that cartoon-voice say. It still makes me want to laugh.

Lake's hair is greasy and glinting in the sun. Her eyes are covered by too-big Gina Lollobrigida sunglasses. Despite the heat, she is wearing all black.

"Hey, Beige."

"My name is Katy," I say.

"Right," Lake says. "But you're still *Beige*."

She just doesn't want to use my name.

She's calling me Beige for a reason.

It's an insult.

I can't imagine that she is visiting me because I was such a great companion at the Fourth of July party. It's more than obvious that she doesn't think I'm cool.

In my mind, I slam the door in her face, go back to my bedroom, pick up my book, and continue reading.

But I don't kick her out. I open the door wider. I let her in.

"What are you doing here?" I ask.

"According to the deal I have with The Rat, I'm supposed to take you 'under my wing,'" she says, coming into the apartment and scanning the place. She sits down on the couch and kicks her long legs on the table.

She's not interested in me. I'm just part of the "deal."

"And what do *you* get out of it?" I ask. And then it hits me. "Are you getting *paid* to hang out with me?"

"Bribed, not paid. It's kind of like a summer job, only not. Besides, everyone I know is . . . at *camp* . . . and you're here for how much longer?"

"Twelve days," I say.

"Exactly my point."

"Why aren't you at camp?" I ask.

I'd rather be at camp. In Rimouski. On a lake that looks like a mirror. In a place where I can see the stars at night. Where there is no smog. A place where if I'm lucky, like I was two years ago, I can lie on a rock near the lake at night and watch the green curtains of light the aurora borealis make as they chase each other across the sky.

"I have better things to do than archery and water sports," she says. "Repeat this to yourself ten times, Beige. Camp is for losers."

The word comes right into my head. A word I don't normally use. BITCH. I want to tell her she's a *bitch*.

"What are we going to do?" I ask instead.

"Shop, for me," she says. "My bribe from your dad was a gift certificate to Guitar Center."

We're sitting on the Number Two bus heading west, and I watch the palm trees go by. They are so tall that they bend like Q-tips, leaning grace-fully in the windless Los Angeles day.

"Does this bus go all the way to the ocean?" I ask.

"Yeah, this is the Two. The Four goes all the way, also," Lake says.

"All the way to the Pacific?"

"No, to the Indian Ocean," Lake says, rolling her eyes. Maybe they will get stuck in the back of her head like that, she does it so often. "Yeah, to the Pacific. The last stop is like one block away."

Let's go to the ocean, I think. Forget about Guitar Center. Let's go dip our feet in the western water, the same water that touches the coast my mother is on. Let's squish our feet in the sand. I haven't even been there yet. Maybe I *want* to go there. Maybe I want to go because The Rat says he never has time to go to the ocean. Isn't that what's supposed to be alluring about Los Angeles? That it's near the ocean? Maybe seaweed will wrap around our calves. Maybe we'll see dolphins. Maybe I'll get freckles. Cute ones. Or sun-kissed blond highlights in my hair. Then I could e-mail Leticia pictures of me all tanned and California cute. That would be something to write home and not be embarrassed about. Let's go to the beach and look at boys who surf. Normal, hot, sporty-looking boys with blond hair and sand stuck on their backs. Boys like Leo. I'm sick of The Rat's neighborhood, being told it's so hipster. Hip is not my aesthetic.

Lake pulls out her iPod and pops her earbuds in so she can freeze me out. Her head bounces up and down. She plays air guitar discreetly in her lap. I stare out the window at the endless strip malls. Los Angeles is the ugliest city I've ever seen.

"Here's our stop," she says, pulling out an earbud and grabbing my hand to pull me off the bus—like I won't be fast enough, like she has to help me keep up or I will be left in the dust.

The bus leaves, tearing off westward. Secretly, I'm still on it. I'm still on my way to the ocean.

When we walk through the sliding-glass doors of Guitar Center, everyone inside is talking in hushed tones, like it's a museum. There are guitars on all the walls behind glass displays. Lake kisses her fingers and then touches the glass in front of one. I hang back a bit and read the name. I don't recognize it. I don't recognize most of the names, and I don't say anything about the few I do because I notice that those are the displays Lake breezes by without so much as a second glance.

We push through to the main room of the store. It's enormous. There are amps on the floor and guitars of every color hanging from every available space on the ceiling. Guitars, guitars, guitars. Green, gold, purple, red, star-shaped, V-shaped, flower-shaped, butterfly-shaped. Crazy. I'm like a kid in the wrong kind of candy store. Instead of being excited, I immediately feel claustrophobic.

"Come on," Lake urges. "We're not stopping here."

She doesn't seem to understand that I don't know where we are going. I'm not a mind reader.

We head out of that room and go up the stairs, to an atrium with a glass display case filled with tons of little gadgets. I can't figure out what the things in the case have to do with guitars. Lake stands there, waiting for a salesman to help us.

I look back over my shoulder, still overwhelmed by the display downstairs. I need to focus on something, so I watch the salesmen with long ponytails, or feathered hair, or dreadlocks, helping people eagerly pick out guitars. How can something be so exciting to so many people yet leave me cold? I mean, I get having music on as, like, background noise, but I could never imagine getting to the point where I'd want to actually perform it, where I'd need all of this equipment and gear. It kind of freaks me out.

I turn and look at Lake. She is trying to catch the eye of a salesperson. I don't get how they don't see her. She's standing right there, leaning against the glass case, practically jumping over it, trying to flag someone down. She's a pretty noticeable person, but amazingly, she seems invisible to them.

A few minutes later, a sales guy happens to look over at me. It's only after he notices me that he sees Lake waving her arms at one of his coworkers who walks right by us. It seems to suddenly dawn on him that maybe we've been trying to get someone's attention. He quickly makes his way over.

"Have you been helped?" he asks me, not Lake. He's young, clean-cut, in a cowboy shirt. My type.

"No. *I* haven't," Lake says, forcing the attention onto her. "And I have been here for like fifteen minutes."

She's not even exaggerating.

"I'm ignored all the time in music stores because I am a girl, and I think that sucks," she informs him.

"I'm sorry," the sales guy says. "We all know that there are women who can rock."

"Oh yeah?" Lake says. "Name your favorite."

He takes a few long seconds to think.

"Well, why don't I tell you who rocks," Lake says, "so you can be schooled. Off the top of my head, I'm thinking Joan Jett, Patti Smith, Liz Phair, Courtney Love, PJ Harvey, Sheryl Crow, Sinéad O'Connor, Aimee Mann, Squid, Gina Volpe, Ani DiFranco, Donita Sparks, Jane Wiedlin, Lita Ford, Chan Marshall, Chrissie Hynde, Nancy Wilson from Heart—you have her guitar out in the front room, FYI." Lake sticks her arm out and points toward the front room, then continues.

"Joni Mitchell, Kim Gordon, Melissa Auf der Maur, Kim Deal, Brody Dalle, Mary Timony. . . . Should I go on?"

The guy smiles.

"No, you've made your point. I've been girl-rock schooled," he says. "I've got one you might like. How about Neko Case?"

"Yeah. Good one," Lake says. "I rock, too."

"I don't doubt it," the guy says.

"Now, let's get down to business. I need a bigger sound, so I could use some help with buying a new pedal. I have the Big Muff, but I'm looking for something crunchier."

Now that the sales guy gets that Lake knows her stuff, he is taking her very seriously. They get into a deep conversation about pedals. They are speaking each other's language. He can tell she is no dabbler. He keeps looking over at me and nodding when he says something technical, including me in the conversation as though I understand what he means. I don't. But I nod back at him and smile.

Now that Lake is being taken seriously, she stands taller. She throws her head around and cops an attitude. More attitude, as if that's even possible. She's in her element, kind of like when Mom talks with her colleagues about the domestic rituals of Incan women.

"You really like Suck, or did you get that T-shirt at a mall?" the sales guy asks.

Lake starts singing some song. I think it's a Suck song called "One, Two, Fuck You." I think they played it the other day. I didn't like that song when I heard it live, and I don't like it acappella here in the store. Those words are frightening. They are so hopeless.

The sales guy joins in and they finish the phrase together.

"It's my dad's shirt. It's original," Lake says.

But she doesn't say *and my dad is Sam Suck*. It seems as though she'd wear that like a neon sign on her forehead. But she keeps quiet about him. She told the guy the truth. It's her dad's shirt. She is standing there throwing respect to her dad, but not using him to get any special treatment.

I wonder. Would I have used The Rat's name if it would help me to get special treatment? Leticia would. I kind of admire that Lake doesn't use Sam's name. She earned the 15 percent discount on her purchases from the sales guy all on her own, just for being herself.

"Next time, Lake, you come straight to me," the sales guy says. "I'll make sure you don't wait."

Lake flicks her hair and shoots him a thumbs-up as we head over to the cashier to make our purchase.

"You just have to show them what's what, Beige," Lake says. "I'll never have a problem with that guy again."

Lake's only coming up to my place 'cause she wants to pee.

"Oh, look," she says. "It's the merman."

She pushes open the gate to the pool and stands on the edge as Leo comes swimming up and hangs on to it.

"What's up, Leo? Get gills yet, fish boy?"

"That's so ha ha funny, Lake," he says. "Still sucking on helium, I hear?"

"I'd rather suck on helium than anything *you* might have to offer," Lake says, and then splashes Leo with her foot. He pushes himself back into the water and moves away from us. I wish he would stay on this side of the pool.

"Come on, Beige, let's leave Needle Dick to his laps," she says.

I cringe. I hope Leo hasn't heard Lake's stupid nickname for me.

"You know him?" I say.

"Yeah, he goes to Marshall High with me. He's on the swim team, on the tennis team, in the Humanities Magnet. Mr. Perfect. I've been in school with him since kindergarten."

I want to tell her that I don't think he has a needle dick because his swimsuit doesn't leave much to the imagination, but I never figured myself to be a total pervert so I close my mouth. It stays sewn shut.

I look back over my shoulder at him. He's paused for a minute from doing his laps and he's looking at us. His eyes catch mine. Is that what a knowing glance looks like? I feel tingly inside.

Maybe I should write Mom and tell her that since coming to Los Angeles, I've become a perv.

It must be The Rat's fault.

WALKING
IN L.A.

MISSING
PERSONS

Letthesunshine: KD! I miss you
sooooooooooooo much! How's LALA land?
Sweetcake: Terrific!

Lame. I'm a liar. I blame Los Angeles for making me one.

Letthesunshine: Sweet! Guess what?!
Sweetcake: Quoi?

Please don't let it be anything fun.

Letthesunshine: Nicolas hooked up with
Holly!

Sweetcake: No way!

Blech. Nicolas is gross.

Letthesunshine: Yeah, but he told me that
Francois told Gaeten that he really liked you.
Sweetcake: Really! Francois likes me!?

François likes me! I'm going home now! I'm going over to Outremont and I'm going to Leticia's basement and I'm going to make out with François.

Letthesunshine: Francois said absence
makes the heart grow fonder.
Sweetcake: Tabernac! I'm coming over to
your house! Now!
Letthesunshine: Run away! Hostie!
Sweetcake: LOL. Gotta jet. I am having too
much fun! I'll be home tres bientot!
Letthesunshine: I'm soooooooo jealous of
you! A tout a l'heure!

I know one thing. I'm missing out on everything.
A message from my mom:

E-mail access at last!! I love getting your text messages. Keep them coming! Your embellished stories are tres drole! I told you Los Angeles was colorful. I can't believe Lake is 16!

I will try to call with the satellite phone as soon as I can. Mountains are beautiful and I'm happy! Our excavation leader is from Italy. The site looks really interesting. I'm so busy. Too much to tell! I'm in absolute paradise! I miss you Katy-bon.
Je t'aime, Maman

The thin mountain air she's breathing must be making Mom light-headed and fuzzy-minded. I can't believe that she's not more anguished about my ten thousand desperate pleas to join her. Shouldn't she be worried that I'm being dramatic? I'm *never* dramatic.

But maybe I was *too* dramatic. Maybe I exaggerated a little too much. I thought that way she'd pay attention and take me seriously.

Instead she thinks I'm being funny.

Or having *fun*.

ROOTS RADICAL

RANCID

The Rat and I are sitting outside at Millie's eating breakfast. We don't say much, The Rat and me; we just eat in silence and drink coffee. I am growing to like the tradition, but I don't tell The Rat that. I like that going out for breakfast gets you out into the world. It is easier than cooking at home in the morning.

"That's a nice shirt," The Rat says to the waiter, breaking the silence.

The waiter shakes hands with The Rat.

"Goodwill."

"Good deal," The Rat says. "I like the color and the snap buttons."

The waiter goes off to get us more coffee.

"He's in a great band. They are like *insane*," The Rat says. "Love their sound."

"His shirt has holes in it."

"So? It still looks good."

If you're homeless, I think.

"Do you want to go thrifting?" The Rat asks. "That could be a fun thing for us to do together."

"No," I say.

"Don't you and your mom go thrifting?"

"Mom and I never shop at *Village des Valeurs*," I say. "We *donate* there."

"Ah. Your mom was a good thrifter, back in the day."

It's hard to imagine Mom wearing used clothing. It's so not her style.

Then I remind myself, it's not her style *anymore.*

A bunch of skater kids whiz by, and my eyes follow them. One of the boys is wearing black kneepads, the baggiest black shorts I have ever seen, black elbow pads, a black T-shirt, and a black helmet. In white letters on the back of his helmet it says GARTH SKATER.

The boys pop their boards into their hands, and when the light turns green, they drop them back down and skate across the street in the little square that has a fountain in it.

I watch them as they do their hanging out thing.

The Garth Skater kid takes a wicked bad fall. The other boys laugh, and Garth gets on his feet and does the trick again. I think that the boys from back home are probably better skaters than these guys. That reminds me that I still haven't heard more from Leticia about François. I'll e-mail her when I get back home. Maybe she'll be online and we can IM. We always seem to be just missing each other because of the time difference. Who knew three hours could create such a big divide between us? I hope she's suffering without me. I know I'm suffering without her. Thank goodness I'm going back to Montréal soon. Nine days and counting . . .

One of the kids skates up to us. He's kind of hovering by our table. It's the kid with the helmet. I stare at him. He nods at me. I don't nod back.

He leans over and taps The Rat on the shoulder.

"Are you The Rat from Suck?" Garth Skater asks.

"Yeah." The Rat lights up.

"Wow, man. You're like, my hero. I mean, like my drumming hero."

"Well, thanks, man," The Rat says.

"I thought it was you. I've seen you at Millie's before, but I was too scared to talk to you. I mean, you know. I wasn't sure."

"Well, it's me," The Rat says.

"I have every single bootleg of Suck. I also have every single version of every song that any band has ever covered of Suck. I mean, you guys are like *the* Los Angeles band."

"Well, thanks," The Rat says.

"I mean, I'm just so honored to be breathing the same air as *The Rat*."

"Well, don't hyperventilate. I'm just a guy like you."

"I'm a drummer, too, you know." Garth Skater air drums intensely and bobs his head up and down and bites on his lower lip. I think it's supposed to show his passion, but it just looks kind of dorky.

He finishes with a fake flourish and bows. The Rat actually applauds.

"Wow, The Rat!" Garth dorkily punches his fists together. Then his skateboard slips from between his knees and rolls away from him.

"Well, see you," The Rat says after Garth as he goes and chases his runaway board. "Oh, and Suck is playing at Sunset Junction. You know. If you're around."

Garth catches his board with one hand and clutches his heart with the other hand and kind of staggers around like he's having a heart attack.

"Are you shitting me?" he asks.

"No, it's true. We're going to start playing out again."

"Oh my God. I've died and gone to heaven," Garth says. "I've got to go post this on my blog."

Then he flicks us the thumbs-up, jumps on his board, and skates away.

"What's Sunset Junction?" I ask.

"It's a street fair."

"I like street fairs," I say. "I want to go to a street fair."

"It's at the end of August," The Rat says.

"Oh. I'll be back in Montréal."

"I know, it's too bad. It's a good time," The Rat says. "Hey, how about we walk over to the Vista and go see a movie? We can get a break from this heat. Sit in some air-conditioning."

"What's playing?" I ask.

"Does it matter?" The Rat asks. "Most movies are crap. Hollywood crap. Made to the lowest common denominator. Made so that people don't have to think."

"So you don't care what's playing?"

"I just care that it's gonna be cold," he says. "And that I'm gonna be with my best girl."

He throws his arm around my shoulder and gives me a squeeze.

His best girl. That's not me. It's Trixie. Or my mom. His best girls are the ones he actually knows. Not me. I'm like a smudge.

Like Lake says. I'm *beige*.

I'm still thinking about how excited that kid was. He was actually freaking out over The Rat. I almost feel bad that I was sitting there having coffee with him and I didn't care.

When we get to the Vista Theatre, The Rat and I go and grab some seats, but there is still some time to kill before the movie starts.

Ask a question. Ask a question.

I'm thinking of all the names I've heard so far. The Punk House. The Yellow House. The

Rockplex. Grunge Estates. It's not just houses either. It's the celebrity Mayfair Market. The Rock-and-Roll Denny's. The Rock-and-Roll Ralphs.

"Why do people refer to your place as Grunge Estates?"

"It's from back in the day," The Rat says, already digging in to the popcorn.

"It's like you guys nickname everything. And everyone."

"It's easier to remember sometimes."

Right, I think. *Like when you're drunk. Or high.*

The lights go down and the curtains open and I am happy for the cold air, the dark theater, the not having to talk, and the being transported out of here. Even if it is only for two hours.

THIS TOWN
THE GO-GO'S

The phone rings. When I pick it up, the line is staticky.

"Hello!"

I feel blubbery. Just hearing Mom's voice makes me all quivery and sad inside.

"Mom! Mom!"

I don't want to lose our connection.

"I'm here! I'm using the satellite phone."

"How's Peru?"

"It's amazing. I wish I could show you the site. It's in pristine condition. Vittorio says that the site is outstanding."

I love her little French accent. It's more pronounced to me now since I haven't talked with her for more than a week.

"I wish I were there," I say. I want to be there. There's still time! I want to ask, *When can I come down to Peru?* I almost ask, but it would be so much sweeter if she asked me.

"How's L.A.?" she asks.

"Ça va," I say. She thinks I can take it. I don't want her to know that I can't. That it's terrible. Get me out of here. You misunderstood my e-mails and text messages. I am *not* having adventures. I miss you.

"And The Rat?" she continues.

I look at The Rat, who's trying to do his own thing and not listen in on my conversation but really is. He's in the doorway of the hall, straightening out a poster.

"He's OK," I say.

"I want a full report," Mom says.

But instead of telling her what is really going on, I come up with things to tell her. I tell her about Millie's and the pool. I tell her about the Suck show and Guitar Center. I tell her about Lake. I try to make everything sound interesting, as interesting as she then makes the dig sound.

It is so good to hear her voice. It's so good that I just let her talk and talk and talk. This is music to my ears.

"The site is really robust," she says at the end. "There's a lot here. I'm really going to have to take my time."

"I'll see you soon. Only eight more days!"

For a minute I think maybe we've been disconnected because Mom doesn't say anything. But the line isn't dead. I can hear more static and Mom's breathing as she kind of sighs before she speaks.

"Well, I think we have to have a change of plans, Katy-bon."

"What do you mean?"

But I know what she means. She already said it. The site is *robust*. She's going to have to take her time.

"I think I'm going to have to stay a bit longer," she says. She says it gently, using the voice that she used to use to tuck me into bed with. It makes me miss her more.

"How much longer?" I try not to sound like a needy baby.

"Well, I need to talk to Beau. It depends on him. I'd like to take as much time here as I can."

I'm quiet. I don't say anything.

"Katy. I won't stay if you don't want me to," she says. "We're a team."

I want to say, *Mom, get on a plane and come back to North America. I am dying here. I am stifled. I am not with my people. I want you back. I want my life back.*

But I am a good girl. A nice girl. I love my mother. I know how much this means to her. To *us*. And the site is *robust*. It's a robust site. And I know what I should say. I can hear it in her voice.

"You should stay," I say. "You should totally stay."

"I knew we were of the same mind about this. I'm so glad you agree, Katy. I think I should stay, too. It's a risk and it's going to cost me so much money, but I think it's worth it. I think my research is really onto something. Vittorio thinks so, too."

She talks more about the site and her thesis and her theory and her site boss, Vittorio, the Italian. She sounds different. Brighter. Happier.

Do I sound different? Or do I sound the same? I know I don't sound desperate enough for her to change her mind and stick with the plan.

When she's done, I pass the phone to The Rat.

"She wants to talk to you," I say. "She has a favor to ask."

"Me?" The Rat says. "She wants something from *me*?"

BEAT ON THE BRAT

THE RAMONES

The Rat enters my room without knocking.

"Oh, shit. I'm sorry," The Rat says. "You could have been naked."

"What?"

"You could've been naked," he says. "Or in here with a boy. I always hated that my parents wouldn't respect my space. Next time I'll wait till you say come in. OK?"

"Yeah."

Then he leaves the room and closes the door behind him. I hear three knocks.

He was already in the room. Why is he making such a big show about this? It's stupid. I make him wait a bit.

"Come in." I say it as though I don't already know he was there. As if it were a surprise.

The Rat comes into the room. He smiles. He's probably pleased with himself for getting it right. He comes over to my desk and sits in the chair. He *rat-tat-tat*s on the desktop. Then he digs into his pocket and pulls out a pick. Then he grabs the guitar from its stand and plucks at it.

I don't know what he wants, and I'm not going to ask, so I go back to reading my book.

"We're going to have to figure out a new plan for you," The Rat finally says, kind of in time to the music. "Suck is going to be practicing a lot, since we're going to give it another go. And that's on top of the other bands I'm in. I've also got some gigs set up that I can't get out of, and I've got to start working again."

He won't stop fiddling with the guitar. It's annoying. "Maybe it's not too late to register you for camp or something," he suggests.

Sleepaway camp, I think hopefully. Or adventure camp. Like *Survivor.* I could have a pup tent and make my own food on a fire. I could eat berries and mushrooms and wild game. You can live off that. I know. I read it in a book.

"In any case, it's going to be *rad* to have you here for the whole summer!" The Rat says.

I nod. I smile. Yeah. It's going to be *great*. I'm trying not to look as unsettled as I feel. Two and a half weeks was OK. The whole summer is *not* OK. How could my mother expect me to be fine with this?

I just want to be away from this room and the piles of crap everywhere and the dirty kitchen. Everything that doesn't feel like home. I just want to transport out of here. I look back down at the words in my book. I can't concentrate on them; they just lie there on the page, promising me an adventure out of here. But I can't focus with The Rat making noise. He's either speaking too much or he's plucking or drumming away.

"Maybe I could get a library card," I say. "I'm running out of books to read." The advantage of having a book is that I can read at the table while I'm eating and look like I am doing something. If I'm reading, then I won't have to talk that much. I can be alone in my own world, block out the real one.

"That's a great idea," The Rat says. Then his

face gets all serious as he plucks out a few notes on the strings. "I think, since you're going to be here awhile, I should tell you that I'm seeing someone."

"Trixie," I say. "I met her and Auggie the other day at the pool."

"Oh."

He kind of bangs on the strings a bit. He looks at the strings and at his hands, but not at me. It's like he can't look up at me. It's like he knows he should have told me.

"You OK with that?" he asks.

I don't say anything until finally he has to look up.

When his eyes meet mine, I shrug.

"I should have told you," he says.

At least he knows it.

"I don't want to jinx it. It's still new. I really like her."

He strums the guitar some more. He hums badly. He should stick to just strumming, or drumming maybe. I want to tell him to get out of my room, because I want to be alone and miserable by myself. I want to tell him to please stop with the humming—it's making me feel worse.

But he just keeps sticking around, like he thinks I need someone in the room with me. Like it's going to comfort me. It's not. The only thing that would comfort me would be my mother coming home and taking me away from here. But that is not going to happen. She is in Peru. I agreed to the new plan. And now I'm not going home.

"Hey, I've got an idea. You know what always makes me feel better?" he asks, not waiting for me to answer. "Pounding the skins. Let's go to the jam space and jam. There is no one there tonight. I'll play drums and you play guitar. It'll be great! All right! I'll just go change into my practice clothes." He places the guitar back onto the stand and runs out of the room to get it together.

Sid Vicious sits in the doorway and lets out a moaning meow.

"Shut up," I say.

Sid Vicious meows again.

I look over at the guitar. It's kind of just staring

at me, making me feel all guilty. I get a knot in my stomach.

"Let's go," The Rat says.

He's pulled on a faded T-shirt that says ADO-LESCENTS, which is fitting because that's what he looks like. He's just standing in my room like some kind of overgrown teenager. But I think Adolescents are a band. I think I saw the name on one of the rock posters in the hallway. Most of his T-shirts are band T-shirts.

"I can't jam with you," I say.

"Can't?" The Rat is proactively putting my guitar in its case because I'm just sitting on the bed not doing anything.

I'm getting madder by the minute that I'm even in this situation at all. If Mom had just stuck to the plan, I could have been gone before he found out.

"Can't," I say.

"Or won't?" he asks.

Suddenly the look on his face is like I'm rejecting him. And I am. Even when he kept trying to check in with his postcards and ill-chosen gifts for me, I could at least keep my distance, because I was far away. And when he was living far away, The Rat seemed unreal to me. But now I can't get rid of him. Now he's right here in front of me with a quizzical look on his face.

I open my mouth. I say it quick, like ripping off a Band-Aid.

"I don't know how to play," I say.

"What do you mean?"

"I mean: *I don't know how to play the guitar.*"

"But I sent you the guitar. I sent you books on how to play the guitar. I sent you DVDs on how to play the guitar. You said—"

"I said thanks, but I didn't say I played."

The Rat lets this sink in.

"Don't you like guitar?"

I shrug.

"OK, OK, maybe guitar is not your instrument. That's cool. I get it. I'm a drummer. Maybe you're a drummer."

"No."

"Keyboards?"

"Nuh-uh."

"Bass?"

"No." I say taking a deep breath. "I guess I don't really like music that much."

He forced me to say it out loud. It's his fault.

The Rat's face turns white. Like maybe he's having a stroke. Then it seems like he swoons, like the women in the novel I'm reading. He actually has to sit down, so he sinks into the chair.

I might need to get some smelling salts for him.

"So, you don't like playing music?" he says. "What about *listening* to music?"

I take the pillow and twist it, like I am strangling it. Only I'm imagining that it's The Rat. I'm not like him. I don't want to be like him. Why doesn't he just leave me alone and stop bothering me?

"Well, listening to music sometimes is OK, I guess. When it's on, like, in a store or a restaurant or in a movie. And there are a few bands I like, when the boys in them are cute. But I prefer quiet. I like to be able to think. I don't know how you can think with all that clatter. Even when there is no actual music playing, there is always noise around here."

I motion toward his hands moving up and down the neck of the guitar case, slapping out an anxious beat. The Rat's hands freeze.

I just should be quiet, but the explanations and

excuses keep spilling out of me, like I've got diarrhea of the mouth.

"Normal people need quiet sometimes," I say.

The Rat always has music on. In the morning, when he gets home, when he gets in the car, when he's in the shower, the first thing he does is turn on the music. I can never get away from it.

"But music is in our blood," he says.

"Sorry, I'm just not that into it," I say. Then I deliver the blow that does it, the one that is really going to shut him up. The one that is going to break his heart. "It's not very *me*."

"OK." He puts his hand up, gesturing for me to stop. Then he gets up slowly and backs out of the room, like I've killed him. Like everything that he ever thought would be cool about having a daughter was wrong. Like he's ashamed that he accidentally created me.

In a minute, I hear him in the living room. He's locked himself into the soundproof closet with his drums. He's closed the door, but I can still hear the dull thud of the thumping beats. He's banging away on his drum kit.

He just keeps banging away for hours.

Like he said, it makes him feel better when he's upset. And by the sound and duration of the banging, he's really upset.

I think about how he looked, as though I told him that I have some kind of incurable disease. And I guess, in his mind, I do.

I am incurably uncool.

WAITING ROOM

FUGAZI

I push my fork around my plate making a mountain out of my Devil's Mess Scramble. Usually it's my favorite thing to order at Millie's, but I'm not really hungry this morning.

"So, I hear that you're going to spend the summer with us here in Los Angeles," Trixie says.

She is eating eggs Florentine, and the green spinach looks gross as it goes into her mouth, against the red lipstick she's wearing.

"Yeah," I say. It feels like she's rubbing it in, even though I know she's not. It feels like if she didn't say it, maybe my staying here for the summer wouldn't be so real. It feels so final when she says it like that, all casual and out loud.

"I'm excited," The Rat says. He acts like he isn't upset or angry or utterly brokenhearted about my disinterest in guitar playing and general dislike of music. Like he's forgotten about the whole thing. Like the drumming worked its magic last night and he's pounded out his disappointment. Even though on our walk over here he told me that it was OK. That he's just never met anyone who doesn't connect with music. So it's weird for him.

"Getting to know you is a bit like learning to speak another language," he said.

Was that supposed to make me feel better?

"I think it's lucky for us," Trixie says, giving The Rat a look. "I, for one, am happy that you're staying. It'll give us more of a chance to get to know each other."

"So, I was thinking," The Rat says, "since I'm going to have to go back to work this week, you might want to take care of Auggie. It'd be something to do."

"You want me to *babysit*?" I say.

I keep pushing my eggs around. No one is saying anything except Auggie. Auggie is babbling up a storm. I look straight at Trixie, who is squirming in her chair.

"This wasn't my idea," she blurts out.

"That's true. It's my idea," The Rat says. "I thought maybe you'd want to make some extra cash, Katy."

There is more silence. I steal another look at Trixie, and she looks like she's mad, too. She's glaring at The Rat.

"What?" The Rat says. "What did I do?"

"Beau, I wouldn't want to be pawned off as a babysitter on my dad's girlfriend on my summer vacation in Los Angeles. There's too much fun to be had. I told you this was a terrible idea. I'm sorry, Katy. I can totally find someone else."

"I was just trying to be helpful," The Rat says. "You need a sitter; here is a teenage girl. Teenage Girl equals Babysitter."

"Ugh," Trixie and I say at the same time.

"Why do you need a sitter?" I ask Trixie.

"My regular girl is taking a summer class that starts next week—Tuesdays and Thursdays. And I work."

"How do you know you can trust me?" I say.

I might be evil. Or irresponsible. Or a witch. I might light candles and say spells. I might have the mark of the devil on me. I don't, but I might.

"You wouldn't even get in the pool without adult supervision. I think I can trust you," she says, and then as an afterthought she adds, "I trust Beau with Auggie all the time."

"I'm pretty good with babies," The Rat says.

"But not so much with diaper changes," Trixie says. "I think you're not good at that on purpose."

"Have you seen what Auggie's packing in those diapers sometimes?" The Rat says.

He's good with babies *now*, I think. Not when I was one. When I was a baby, he just wasn't interested. He just wasn't there.

"Good thing you know how to cook," Trixie says, grabbing The Rat's hand. "Have you made Katy your pasta puttanesca yet?"

"No. Not yet," The Rat says.

"Well, you should. Mmmmm."

As Trixie and The Rat talk, they give each other looks that say *I'm sorry* and *I forgive you* all at once. They are a team. If I'm going to be stuck in this town for the summer, then I don't want to be left out. I want to say, *How come you never cook for me? How come you just hand me the take-out menus? Why are we always ordering in or going out?*

Instead I say, "Fine, I'll sit for you."

F**K ARMAGEDDON... THIS IS HELL

BAD RELIGION

Lake is lying on my bed plucking away on my guitar. She is sporting her usual outfit of black jeans and a tight T-shirt. She wears black every time I see her pretty much. It makes her look kind of doom and gloomy.

Lake pauses her guitar noodling to pull the pink and purple knit blanket from my bed and wrap it around herself, like she just got a chill, even though it's one hundred million bagazillion degrees outside.

I don't want her wrapping my blanket around herself. She smells like BO because she doesn't wear deodorant or shave her armpits. It's my mom's blanket, and it still kind of smells like her perfume.

"So, The Rat tells me you're staying all summer," Lake says.

Fact. She's just stating the facts. I just nod because if I say yes, I know I'll start to cry, and I don't want Lake to see me cry.

"Guess I'll be getting a bigger bribe," Lake says.

Bitch, I think.

"Yep. Guess so," I say.

Lake smiles. She seems as if she's going to make another bitchy comment. Then she looks at me, and for a second, her face softens. I think I see in her eyes, behind that look, that she's saying, *Hey, Beige, I understand disappointment. I understand.*

But then the moment is gone and I'm left wondering if I made it up. I look up at her again, though, just to make sure. But now she doesn't look sorry for me at all. She's just plucking away at my guitar. She is probably just glad she can get another piece of equipment at Guitar Center. I'm not quite sure why she keeps coming over and then just sits there, kind of ignoring me and playing my guitar. Doesn't she have anything better to do?

I put my nose back into my book. I can't read while she's just sitting here in my room. Just plucking away. Just casually ruining my mother's blanket.

I want her to stop playing, which means I'll have to distract her from the guitar, and that means talking. I need to get her talking so she'll stop playing.

"So, what's your band called?" I ask.

She gets into the I'm-getting-comfortable-now-because-I-can-talk-about-my-favorite-subject, ME, pose.

"The Grown-Ups," she says, and sticks out her boobs, displaying the name emblazoned on her T-shirt. "We're great. This is my new T-shirt design. I silk-screened it myself."

The blanket slides a bit off her shoulder, and so she yanks it back up. Then she looks at me, and I can tell she can see that I'm annoyed.

"What's your problem, Beige?"

I'm caught. What can I say to be polite? I'm blank. I am at a loss for words.

"My mom made that blanket," I say. "It still smells like her."

Lake looks at me like she doesn't care.

I tell the truth.

"I miss her," I say quietly.

"Oh."

She pulls on the edge of the blanket and it falls off her shoulders. I pull it toward me. I want my mother's blanket to comfort *me*. That's why I brought it with me to Los Angeles. I want it around *my* shoulders. Maybe I am getting ready to talk about *me*.

But I'm not. I don't open my mouth and tell her that my mom made it for me when she was in rehab. When she was pregnant with me. That my mom made a blanket big enough for a king-size bed because she was freaking out, and knitting was the only thing that kept her from not losing her mind while the junk was leaving her body and I was growing bigger and bigger inside of her each day.

She knit then. Everyone she knew then got a knit blanket when she was in rehab, she said. She doesn't knit now. Even though a bunch of her friends have a knitting circle. Even though I keep asking her to teach me. Even though Leticia says it would be cool to know how to knit and we should totally learn how.

"That was then, Katy," Mom says. "I knit all I had in me."

I pull the blanket closer around me. A silence emerges between Lake and me. A pause hangs in the air, a pause in me and a pause in her that meets in between us.

Lake puts the guitar down on the bed. She looks at her hands, stretches them out, and then balls them into two fists. She talks to her hands.

"My mom died one month after coming home from rehab," Lake says.

I just stare at her. It's something we have in common. Our mothers were junkies. It dawns on me. They were junkies *together.*

"It happens a lot like that, one last ride before you kick for real," Lake says.

I remember to speak.

"No one ever told me that," I say. I don't say *I'm sorry.* Or *That's terrible.* Somehow I feel like if I did say that, I would incur Lake's wrath. And I don't want to feel angry right now. I want to breathe in my mom's scent from the blanket.

"Yeah. The thing is that you can't handle the same amount you were using before rehab," she says. "My mom had two of those blankets that your mom knit for her."

"Really?"

"I have one, too. A small one. I was a baby when your mom left."

Lake stands up and gently puts the guitar back on the stand.

"I gotta go," she says.

"OK," I say. And as an afterthought, I add, "I'll talk to you later."

I know right then that I can't be that mad at my mom anymore for staying in Peru. She may be far away, but at least she didn't leave me for good.

I go into the living room, and The Rat is lying on the couch with earphones on. He's plugged into the stereo. His foot is bouncing up and down to a rhythm I can't hear. I stand there until he notices me. He pulls one earphone off his head, and now I can hear the music all tiny and tinny blaring out of it.

"What's up?" The Rat asks.

I shrug.

He sits up. He pulls off the other earphone and then flips off the stereo so that there is silence.

"You hungry?"

I shrug.

As I sit, I pull on the knit blanket that covers the back of the couch.

"Did Mom make this?" I ask.

"Yeah," The Rat says. "When she was in rehab. I think she needed a hobby to keep her hands busy."

I nod.

"Did you have a hobby?" I ask. "I mean, after you left rehab?"

The Rat laughs and points up at all the model airplanes on the ceiling.

"How long have you been clean?"

"I've been clean five years now," he says. "Five years and counting."

"Was it hard? Kicking?"

"Yeah," The Rat says.

"Did you know Lake's mom died after being in rehab?"

"Sure. Her dying was the beginning of me getting clean. It was hard for me not to shoot up after I checked out of rehab, too," he says. "But I didn't. I didn't."

"Do you think it was hard for Mom?"

"Oh, Katy. Do you know how much your mom loves you?"

I nod.

I close my eyes and I take a deep breath. I'm tired from all the heavy thinking, so I lean my head on The Rat's shoulder.

He smells like cigarettes and sweat.

LIVE FAST DIE YOUNG

CIRCLE JERKS

The Rat finishes his omelet and drains his cup of coffee. Then he readjusts his tiny cowboy hat, lets out a big sigh, and picks up his toolbox from the floor. He jerks his thumb for me to follow him. He settles up the bill, and we head out the door.

"I gotta go to work. You going to be OK on your own?" he asks.

"Yeah," I remind him. "I'm almost fifteen."

"Right, you're a young lady," The Rat says, kind of chuckling to himself. Like he thinks it's funny. It's not.

He needs to be told it's no joke. I *am* a young lady.

"Mom let me go to the Mont Royal Tam-Tams with Leticia by ourselves last year."

He shudders.

"Drum circles aren't my thing," he says, looking kind of grossed out. "OK then. Have a good day."

He walks away from me, but he keeps turning back and looking at me standing on the corner, like he's terrified that he's actually leaving me alone. Like he thinks I can't handle being by myself. If he knew me, he'd know I prefer it. When he gets to his car, he looks back at me one last time.

I wave. I want to say, *God, it's not like you're leaving me forever now. You already did that. Don't act all worried and guilty about leaving now. You left me when I was a baby. I don't expect you to come back.*

I walk down to Sunset Boulevard and explore the neighborhood, by myself. On the way there, I pass that guy I always see walking everywhere in the neighborhood. He's either reading or listening to a little radio or talking on his cell phone. He ignores me when I nod politely to him.

On Sunset there are four cafés, a florist, a cheese shop, a bunch of clothing stores, and a bunch of furniture stores. If I had money, I could spend it really easily. Maybe babysitting for Trixie isn't such an awful idea.

No.

Wait.

It is awful.

My summer job could have been making discoveries relevant to the study of civilization. And now I'll be changing diapers.

One of the clothing stores has all old vintage clothes. I don't want to go in there. The salesgirl seems like she'd laugh at anything I looked at. Besides, it's a bit too funky for me in there. But outside on the sidewalk there is a five-dollar sale rack. That's pretty cheap. I could get a lot of stuff for five dollars. I could just check it out. I pull through the clothes, even though I'm sure there's nothing here I would wear. But there is no harm in looking. I'm holding onto a pale-pink beaded sweater when I look up and I see him coming toward me. Leo. He's reading an extreme sports magazine. He's going to pass right next to me.

I'm prepared.

I lift my hand up and I say, "Hello!"

He doesn't even slow down. He doesn't even look up. He totally ignores me and just keeps walking.

"Hi!" someone says back. I look over the rack of clothing.

It's that kid with the helmet. I read his name again. Garth Skater.

"You're The Rat's kid, right?" he says. "How are you? That is so cool that you remembered me. I didn't think you'd remember me."

He licks his finger and scores himself a one in the air.

I wasn't even saying hello to him. I then kind of want to remind him that he's wearing a helmet! With his name on it! Who wouldn't remember him?

"What's your name again?" he asks.

I don't want to tell him my name. It's none of his business. But he's looking at me so expectantly. I guess I should say something.

"Beige," I say.

He furrows his brow, like he doesn't understand me.

"Beige," I say a little louder. The name feels strange on my tongue.

"*Oh!* I get it! It's ironic! 'Cause you're so cool! *Nice.* I like it. Beeeeeeeeeigggggggggge!"

He makes his hand surf the air in front of him as he says it.

"Anyway, see ya," I say, and I walk away. I'll head to the Los Feliz Library. It'll be a cool escape in there. And there are computers. I've decided to go through all the classics they have in the teen section. I'm going to start on the letter zed and go backward. Why start at the beginning? I bet no one ever actually gets to zed. I kind of feel bad for zed. I'll be the girl that loves zed.

"Hey, wait up! Beige!"

I don't turn around at first, because I forget that I told him Beige was my name.

"Yo!" Garth skates up to me.

"Yeah?" I say.

"Wanna hang out sometime?" he says.

He blurts it out. Unsmooth. Is he asking me out? I don't want *him* to be asking me out. That's not right. Then again it doesn't *feel* like he's asking me out, like a boy asks out a girl. It feels safe. It feels like he just wants to be friends with me. Maybe he just wants to hang out with me because of The Rat. No one has ever wanted to be friends with me because of that reason. I wonder if he's using me. He doesn't *look* like a user.

I shrug.

"OK, great!" he says. "That's wicked! I'm around here all the time 'cause I'm taking drum lessons at the Silverlake Conservatory of Music. Actually I'm late for my lesson. So, you know, cool! I'll see you!"

And then he skates awkwardly away.

What a mess he is! He didn't even ask for my number. He doesn't even know how to get in touch with me. He's the biggest loser I've ever met. Even bigger than me.

And now he thinks my name is *Beige*.

SHEENA IS A PUNK ROCKER

THE RAMONES

I meet Lake by the entrance of what looks like a crappy garage. There's an angel hanging over the entrance. She takes one of the million keys from her key ring and opens the door.

There is musical stuff everywhere—instruments, racks of guitars, two drum kits, five amps, and a piano. A minifridge sits in the corner, and rock-and-roll action figures are strung up from the ceiling along with blue Christmas lights. There's a beat-up couch against the wall.

"First things first," Lake says. "Don't touch any of my shit. Or at least ask first. This is, like, my sacred space. And never, *ever* touch my guitars."

"Don't worry—I don't want to touch your guitars."

I don't even want to touch my *guitar*, I think.

"Good, then I've communicated my feelings and now we have an understanding about it," Lake says.

Is she joking? She didn't communicate anything to me except that she's bossy.

I sneak a peek at the guitars. I don't want to look at them too long, 'cause I bet she'd think that my even looking at them too long would hurt them.

I can picture Lake rocking out and picking up one of her guitars and smashing it into a million pieces. I bet she's that kind of person, the kind of person who smashes a guitar to emphasize her point. She probably gets it from Sam Suck. It's a gene I was born without. I wonder how hard it would be to smash a guitar. I wonder which one on the wall would break the easiest. I'm measuring them all with my eyes.

"This is my jam space," she continues. "This is where I come when I need to create or when I can't take my grandma anymore. It's like my fortress of solitude. You know, when I need to be on my own."

She closes her eyes for a second and does a Zen breath.

"Don't you live with your dad?" I ask.

She gives me a look, so I know she thinks it was a dumb question.

"There are no dumb questions," Mom says. "Questions are points of entry to inquiry. And inquiry is the road to knowledge."

"For years my dad could barely take care of himself. You think he could take care of me?" she says. "Want a Coke?"

That's a question I can answer.

"Sure," I say.

She opens the minifridge and grabs us Cokes. She throws me mine and I barely catch it. Lake laughs.

"That wasn't too graceful."

I shrug. Usually I'd be embarrassed, but something about the space makes it OK to be clumsy. I open the Coke and take a long sip. It buys me time to think.

"You know, I've never taken anyone here who wasn't a musician or here to jam," she says.

"Why?" I ask.

"I don't usually mix with civilians," Lake says.

"Civilians?"

"Anyone who doesn't play music." Lake turns her back on me and busies herself with something.

I look around again at the space. It's messy, but the mess doesn't bother me. It makes sense here. The place has a certain feel to it. I can't put my finger on it. Maybe it's that, civilian or not, somehow I don't feel judged.

Lake picks up one of the guitars and starts playing it. It sounds kind of nice. It sounds like I'm dreaming. But I don't say that. I just let her keep playing and singing mumbly-like to herself. I watch her as her sturdy hands move along the neck of the guitar. Her hair spills over her face and her brow is crinkled, concentrated. I notice that she has blond roots growing out. She's really a California blonde! That makes me want to laugh. But she would hate it if I laughed, so I won't. But she looks soft as she plays. She looks nice, even pretty.

She catches me staring at her. She glares back.

"It's not a song or anything. I'm just noodling. It helps me to think," Lake says. I don't know why she has to eyeball me like she's angry. Then she starts playing again, and the notes she pairs together fill up the air between us.

I take my book out of my bag and put my nose in it. I try to concentrate on the words, but the words Lake whispers to herself as she continues to noodle keep mingling with the words I'm reading in the book and they don't go together. I don't want to be listening, but I am. Mostly I don't want Lake to know I'm listening. So I just make it look like I'm reading. But really, I'm relaxing, maybe for the first time since I got to Los Angeles. I can breathe. I do it. I take a deep breath.

After a bit Lake stops with her strumming and mumbling half-singing and says, "You want to jam before the others get here?"

I give up pretending to read. I put my book down.

"I don't play, remember? Music is not my thing."

"Too bad," Lake says. She noodles a bit more, and I watch her fingers on the neck of the guitar. Her fingers are long. They lazily press the strings, caressing them, really, and the result of the caress is always the same thing: music.

"So, what is your *thing*?" she asks.

"I have no *thing*," I say. Why does everybody think that every single person has to have a thing?

"Lame. I'd die without music. I'd just die." She plays some more. I close my eyes. I realize it's not the music that I like. No. It's the sense of liberation in this space. Like the air in here is clearer. Or there is more oxygen so you can really be alert.

"You know, most of the people I play with, they pretend to like music, but it's just a bullshit thing to them," Lake says. "At least you're honest about not being that into it."

I open my eyes and look at her. She's being serious with me. Like the room has cast a spell on her, too. A nice spell.

One thing I've noticed is that when I'm quiet, other people just start talking and spilling out their secrets. I want to confess something, too, but I can't think of anything to say.

"They're, like, just visiting music," she continues. "They don't take it seriously. They do it more for the look. But I don't care—I'm going to take over the world. This winter I'm going to record. Next summer, I'm going to go on tour. Mark my words. Tour equals adventure time."

I guess that's what every musician calls it: adventure time. Everything I know about rock tours comes from The Rat's postcards. Bad food and hours on the highway, long stretches away from home. That doesn't sound adventurous to me. It sounds terrible. I'm away from home and I don't feel like I'm on adventure time. But I'd like to be the kind of girl who goes on an adventure. Peru would have been adventure. Why there and not here?

"There's an all-ages show later. Wanna go?" Lake asks.

I'm not really paying attention when I nod. I actually say yes.

"Cool," she says, like it's nothing. No big deal that I said I'd go to a show. Like it was the expected answer. But me, I feel jittery and nervous. Like I've agreed to do something that will get me into trouble. This place feels as though any thing, any thought is possible. Dangerous thoughts. New thoughts. Before I have time to back out, the door opens up and the other members of her band start trickling in.

They are a different kind of girl than Lake. It surprises me. They look like they belong in a different band, not her band. They look like the punk you see in magazines, not dressed down like Lake is.

"Who's that?" one of the girls asks Lake, flicking her glitter-lidded eyes over to me.

"Beige," Lake says. "She's The Rat's kid. She's visiting for the summer. She's going to do our merch."

She doesn't say I'm a friend. She makes it sound like I'm a drag. Since I sound like a drag, the girls look like they feel sorry for Lake. They look back over at me.

I sink deeper into the couch, so deep I stab myself in the back with a broken spring. I try to make myself invisible with my book held up as a barrier while they all strap their instruments on, flip on the amps, and begin jamming.

The music here is not just a soundtrack in the background. Somehow the notes flowing together lead to new waves of thinking. I can't help it. I'm listening.

Immediately, the spell the jam space cast on me is broken. It's too loud. I can't concentrate on anything else but them as Lake sings into the mic.

"You're so lost,
And I'm so found,
And I know now
To stop hanging around.
Listen to what I say—
IT'S OVER.
GO AWAY.

I will be beastly
Next time you see me.
I'll show no mercy
Next time you're with me.
Listen to what I say—
IT'S OVER.
GO AWAY."

Lake's baby-girl voice is surprisingly powerful when she sings. But I don't like when she screams. She isn't afraid to jump with her guitar, to smash and rub the strings. When her lips come up to the microphone to sing, it's like she's kissing it. Her mouth opens and it's sexy. She doesn't look like a girl; she looks like a fearless woman. Roaring. Then she jerks back and concentrates on the guitar, turning her back against the mic she was just making a kind of love to, and crouches low, fingers flying along the fret board.

Despite what Lake says, the other girls don't seem like they're faking their enthusiasm. They seem like they're totally into it. They sound just as serious as she does about it. They sound like they're making good music. Even though I don't really know what good music sounds like, at least I can sort of understand the lyrics. Not like Suck, where I couldn't understand a single word. Lake doesn't sing like she has marbles in her mouth.

I just know my foot taps without any effort at all.

SEARCH AND DESTROY THE STOOGES

I was going to bail out of going to the show with Lake until the other girls in the band said they were too busy to come and then I felt obligated.

"We don't have to see every band," one of the girls, the one named Kim, whined.

"Well, I do," Lake said. "Come on, Beige."

I think we are going to a club, but it's actually a show at the Armenian Recreation Center. Kids of all ages are everywhere outside. It's a whole scene. It reminds me of the Fourth of July barbecue, only at least here everyone is closer to my age. It doesn't make a difference, though. I still don't fit in.

"I can't get them to do anything outside of practice," Lake complains. "And they barely ever do that. It sucks."

I watch Lake as she sticks her hand out to the ticket guy to get a wristband and I do the same. I know I look plain in my Le Tigre shirt and capri pants. How is it that her dressed down is punk, and mine makes me look like I don't belong? How does that work?

"You don't look punk," I say. "Like what I thought punk was."

"Oh, is there a punk look?" she asks, raising an eyebrow.

"Yeah, like a Mohawk or something. Plaid pants," I say. "Like the girls in your band."

"You don't know shit," she says. "You can't just go into a Hot Topic and buy a costume and be punk. It's more than that."

I shrug.

"So what is it?" I ask. "What's punk?"

She shoots me a look.

"You need to figure it out for yourself," Lake says.

I hate the way she always tries to shut me up. Shut me down. I hate more that I don't know anything.

Why *can't* she just tell me?

As soon as the band comes on, Lake shoves her way to the front. I follow her. I don't want to be left alone in an ocean of people I don't know.

Lake leans forward so she's draping half her body onto the stage. I hang back behind her. People push up against me, bumping me into Lake's back, so I keep saying "I'm sorry" and "Excuse me," but then I realize that everyone is on top of each other, and no one is being polite about personal space, except me. So I stop apologizing.

The light plays on Lake's face, changing from yellow, to blue, to red, to green, her eyes half open during some songs, her mouth moving, her face holy. Like she's in church. Everyone around us has the same expression. I turn around and look at the ocean of people behind me, moved by the musical spirit.

I just don't get it. To me it's too much noise and too much sweat from too many bodies too close together.

I watch the singer as he jumps around and pushes himself off the monitors. I watch the bass player bouncing around with his perfectly rock-floppy hair and two front teeth made of gold. I listen hard; I feel the music pounding in my chest. What is it about this band that makes the bass player jump and the crowd sing along?

Three other bands take the stage, and then the last one plays a bunch of encores. I think they're never going to stop, but then thankfully, they do, and the show is over.

"I'm going to get a T-shirt," Lake says, and splits. She's probably still mad at me because of my faux pas. I am alone as the crowd starts to move around me, dispersing. Socializing.

I notice that Lake is standing near the merch table, handing out something to people passing by.

"Hey!" a girl next to me says. "How'd you like the show?"

Why is she talking to me? I don't think I know her. I don't think she is in Lake's band. They said they had better things to do.

"It was OK," I say. OK is neutral. Noncommittal.

"I thought it was *awesome*."

I shrug.

"Beige, it's Garth," the girl finally says. "Garth Skater."

I have to readjust my eyes to change the gender of this pretty girl in front of me into a boy.

"You probably didn't recognize me without my helmet on," he says.

"Yeah, that must be it." I don't want to tell him it's because I thought he was a girl. He is really pretty. Too pretty. Not boy pretty. He should keep his helmet on. It's less distracting.

"I totally spaced on getting your number or anything. You know, to hang out."

"Yeah," I say.

"But I guess we're hanging out now!" he says. He nods to someone waving hello, to people who are passing us by. They don't seem to really acknowledge him, but it doesn't stop him from making an effort to be social to everyone.

"Yeah," I say.

I want to ask him where his helmet is. I think I feel more comfortable when he has it on. I don't ask him, though. I just keep staring at the top of his head. I focus on his brown-blond curls, trying not to notice his long, long eyelashes, his smooth girlish skin, his high cheekbones, his pouty lips. He is prettier than I could ever hope to be. I'm kind of jealous.

I don't find him attractive like I find Leo attractive. Garth Skater doesn't do it for me. He's just so girl-pretty I can't help kind of staring at him.

"What. Do I have something on my face?" Garth asks.

He starts taking his hand and rubbing at his chin.

"Did I get it?" he asks. He looks really concerned. "I don't want to look stupid. Be honest with me, Beige. Is it gone?"

I nod. He smiles. Out of the corner of my eye, I notice Lake waving at me from next to the merch table.

"Oh, *snap*, Beige! Are you friends with Lake Suck?" Garth asks.

I nod. Nodding makes it not really a lie. Right?

"Holy shit, you are like the coolest girl I know," he says, and then he starts bowing to me, like I'm a goddess and he's worshipping me.

He must not know a lot of girls if he thinks I'm the coolest one he knows.

"I gotta go," I say.

"Meet me tomorrow at Casbah!" he says. "Like elevenish."

I nod OK. It's not really saying yes. It's more like having a spasm. And a spasm could mean anything.

144

I leave him and join Lake as he does a little victory dance.

"Who's your girlfriend?" Lake says.

"Some kid who lives around me, I think," I say. "His name is Garth Skater."

"Oh, him? He's a pain in my ass."

"You know him?" I say. "He doesn't seem so bad."

"I see him at school and at all the shows. But I don't talk to him."

Surprise, surprise, I think. Does Lake actually talk to anyone?

Come to think of it, I've only ever seen her talk to me.

"Did you give him a Grown-Ups sticker?" she asks.

"No," I say.

"Why not?" she asks.

"I don't have any," I say.

She shoves a bunch into my hand.

"Get to work," she says. "We've got promoting to do."

ROCK THE CASBAH

THE CLASH

I slink into a seat outside at the Moroccan-style café called the Casbah. I order a yerba maté because it is very South American and I imagine that my mom is having one right now. I picture her as she finishes drinking it, puts the cup on the shelf in the tent, and goes outside and begins to bend her fingers into the earth as she digs through history.

My fingers dig through an *Entertainment Weekly*. It's not quite the same thing.

Garth skates up to me, giving me a big dumb wave. As he approaches, he jumps off his board. He's wearing his helmet. He doesn't take it off. Secretly, I'm glad.

"I was kind of worried that you wouldn't show," Garth says.

"I had no plans today," I say. I play it as though I *always* have plans. I don't say I don't have any plans these days. Besides babysitting, my calendar is totally free, which is why I even got here *early*.

"Yeah, well, a lot of people are flakes," Garth says. "They say one thing, but they do another. I always *do* what I *say* I'm going to do."

"Always?"

"Yeah," he says. "I'm a man of my word."

Boy. *Boy* of his word, I think, as he goes over to the counter and orders a coffee. There is nothing about Garth that I would call *manly*. He spills some of his coffee on the floor on his way back to join me at the table. He makes an angry-with-himself face. I feel bad; he was walking so slowly and smoothly and yet he still couldn't keep it from spilling.

I bet that is his lot in life, always spilling things, always tripping and falling. He's done something like that every time I've ever seen him.

Garth removes his messenger bag off his shoulder and that's when I notice it.

He has a *boner.*

I want to say, *What is that?* I want to point to his crotch.

"What?" he says.

He follows my eyes. Then he gets two red spots on his cheeks. He's really embarrassed. "It won't go down," he says quietly. "I'm not hot for you or anything. It's biological."

"That's weird," I say. I want to be the kind of girl who's not embarrassed. But I am. I really am. It's just there in front of me. Eye level. I wish he'd sit down so I wouldn't have to see it anymore.

"It doesn't mean anything," he says, kind of whispering. He finally quickly takes his seat. "I'm just nervous. If I liked you, or if I were facing bodily harm, I'd lose it."

"Really? Isn't it supposed to work the opposite way?" I am whispering now too.

"Yeah. I have no control over it," he says, shaking his head, trying to shake it off, trying to play it cool, like it doesn't matter. "I have no game. I'm probably going to be a virgin forever."

The waitress comes over with the triple-decker sandwich and soup that he's ordered. For a skinny boy, he's ordered a lot of food.

"I've never seen you around before," Garth says. "I mean, I have seen The Rat around for like, ever, but I've never seen you. What school do you go to?"

"I live in Canada. In Montréal."

"Do you speak French?"

Garth is the only person so far here who knows that French is a language spoken in Canada.

"Oui," I say.

"Cool. *J'apprends à parler le français à l'école,"* he says with not too bad an accent. "I already speak Spanish. I aspire to be trilingual."

He takes a big bite out of his sandwich, so we're quiet while he chews with his mouth open.

"So, what's it like?" he asks when he's done.

"What?" I say.

"Canada. The Great White North."

"Different."

"How?" He smiles.

He pushes his plate of food toward me and indicates that I should eat something. I take an olive and put it in my mouth.

"I dunno. The food tastes different."

"It does?" he says. I wish he'd shut his mouth when he chews.

"Yeah, it's got more flavor. Everything here seems, like, bland."

"Trippy."

"Yeah. I guess."

"And you have *winter*," he says.

"Yeah."

"Do you live in an igloo?"

"Ha. Ha."

"Hang out with Eskimos?"

"They are called Inuit," I say.

"I've never seen snow fall in my life."

"Never?" I ask. That just seems incredible to me.

"Yeah. I mean, I've seen snow. On the ground. Or on those mountains over there. And I've seen it falling in movies, but I've never seen it fall in real life."

"Well, it gets really quiet during a snowstorm. And it kind of warms up a bit. And in Montréal, it's cold enough that they make, like, homemade ice rinks in the park. But it gets really cold. And dark super early. It's actually kind of depressing."

"Sounds nice," Garth says. "I'm going to put Montréal on my list of places to visit."

"Yeah, it's a good place."

We don't say anything for a little bit. We just kind of sit there.

I am lost in my thoughts about my fake temporary home. Now that I'm staying for the summer, I might try Garth out as a friend. I can't pretend to have fun for two months with no one to hang out with, and since I don't have that many options, I do like Mom says. I don't look a gift horse in the mouth.

Finally Garth says, "I'll wear tighter pants if that makes you feel more comfortable."

That seals the deal. He's kind of a keeper.

I WANNA BE YOUR DOG

THE STOOGES

I'm lying by the side of the pool, my feet dangling in the water, looking up at the sunset. The sky is orange. Orange like an explosion. The light that falls on me makes my pale skin look tan.

"They call it the magic hour," a voice behind me says.

It's Leo.

He's standing right above me, his bare feet almost stepping on my hair. His legs are shaved, a bit stubbly. His bathing suit, blue, doesn't hide much.

I can't breathe.

"You can swim if you want. I'm a lifeguard."

Then, with the grace of a dolphin, he bends his legs and springs forward, diving right over me.

For one half second he is parallel to my body. My heart beats wildly.

When he hits the water, the drops fly back and splash me.

I sit up and watch his long arms break the water as he does laps.

The sky has changed in a matter of seconds. The streetlights flicker on with a buzz, set off by the dipping sun.

Leo swims up to me. He puts his hands on my calf, then he pretend pulls, like he's going to pull me in.

"Psych," he says. His teeth are very white. Does he bleach them? Or does he just have good teeth? Who cares? They are perfect. Perfectly pearly-white teeth set in a perfect smile.

"You coming in?" he asks.

It is still hot despite the fact that the sun has set. The air is still. I slide into the pool. I begin to tread water, but I get tired. I hang on to the edge, to steady myself. Leo has continued with his swimming.

I hang on to the side and watch him. The water makes his arms and legs glisten, slick, wet. He swims half the length of the pool, and on the way back, he glides up my body, presses up against me, his arms around me. Pool water in his mouth, he spits it out on top of my head, slowly, like he's a fountain, and then laughs a little. His skin is touching mine, his legs sliding over mine.

My heart is pounding.

I think he's going to kiss me. He leans in close like he's going to. Instead he says all low-like, "You're all wet."

Then he laughs again, and pushes away from me and swims away.

I think I'll die.

"Beige. Get out of the pool."

It's Lake. Suddenly, she's right there.

Leo eyes us from the other side. He juts his chin out in a greeting to Lake, then he dives under the water and swims almost the entire length of the pool.

I'm shivery. I climb out of the water.

"He's not your type," Lake says as she hands me my towel.

"I don't know what you're talking about," I say.

I close the gate to the pool, but I look back over my shoulder at Leo as he continues to swim.

His body is dissected into parts by his strokes and by the lines he makes as his arms and legs disappear under the water.

Head. Shoulders. Arms. Back. Bum. Legs.
Beautiful.

(I'M) STRANDED

THE SAINTS

Trixie has asked me to come over so I can get acquainted with the apartment before I babysit for Auggie. I don't even have to come over—she said it was *no big deal* and that she *trusted me,* but I am a good girl and, like Garth, I keep my word. I said I'd come over before I started sitting, so come over I do.

I knock on the door.

Trixie sticks her head out and puts her finger up to her lips.

"Auggie's finally sleeping."

The first thing I notice is that she looks great dressed in denim jeans, a 1940s shirt, and her black hair pulled back in a red bandana. She looks like the woman in that World War II poster, Rosie the Riveter. The second thing I notice is the whole place is filled with mermaids. Mermaids of every kind. And blue. The apartment is all kinds of blue.

"I'm kind of obsessed," Trixie says. "I always liked that story. When I was young."

"'The Little Mermaid,'" I say.

"Yeah, but the real version. The sad one," she says. "Not the Disney one."

She shows me around, and I can barely hear her because the stuff in her apartment is more interesting than what she's saying.

"Oh, and you can touch anything or try anything on. I always hated when adults would be freaked out about me touching cool shit. I have a lot of cool shit. If you break anything, well, I'll be really bummed. But I'll still have plenty of other cool shit."

Immediately my hand reaches out and strokes two enormous plumed fans on the wall. I love that I can touch anything. I love that Trixie has no rules.

"Cool, huh?" she says.

I stroke the feathers.

"They're soft."

"They were Misty Temple's. She was a burlesque queen in Los Angeles in the teens. I perform in this modern burlesque show once a month. Wanna see my feather dance?"

I nod.

Trixie removes the feather fans from the wall. She puts them on her couch as she moves some furniture around. She grabs a CD and puts it on, volume low. As the music fills the air, Trixie takes the feathers and opens them up and starts to dance.

"Imagine I'm just wearing pasties and a little G-string," she says. "Of course, Misty Temple was really nude. But you can't be nude in the revue that I'm in."

Her body moves and gyrates as she wiggles in and out of the feather fans, never really showing more than her face. The feathers cover her gracefully. It's mesmerizing.

"Wow," I say.

"Want to learn?"

"Me?"

"Yeah, you could learn to do the feather dance. I used to do it in the burlesque show. It was my act, but now I'm doing this Cleopatra thing. I like to switch it up. For a while I did a total mermaid thing. Come on, I'll show you how to hold them."

She puts them in my hand and begins to show me how to twist my wrist.

"They're heavy," I say.

"It takes a lot of strength to make it look effortless," Trixie says. "That's the big secret."

She starts to sway next to me and I copy her as I move my body. I start to sway. She makes her hips, her arms, her shoulders, her legs pop and bend to the accents in the music. Trixie helps me twist and sway, occasionally putting a hand on my body to move me in the right direction.

Do boys like this? Would Leo?

I twist and dance more, kind of imagining eyes are on me. Leo's eyes. I feel a little tingly.

"That's it! You're a natural! Burlesque is all about feeling sexy and being titillating," Trixie says. "It totally gets your dad hot."

Ew. Suddenly I don't want her touching me. I don't want her twisting with me the way she might twist to get The Rat all hot and bothered. I stop dancing, but the music continues without me.

Auggie's voice crackles through the baby monitor. Trixie smiles.

"He's awake!" she says.

I follow her into the other room as she takes him up into her arms.

"Look, Auggie—it's Katy! She's your new babysitter! Isn't she pretty?"

Auggie hides his face in her shoulders. Shy.

"He's just shy around new people. He just doesn't want to be away from me."

Me and Auggie, we feel the same.

I want to tell him. Warn him. That moms might leave for two weeks and stay away for two months.

I DON'T WANNA HEAR IT

MINOR THREAT

"Did it go well at Trixie's?" The Rat asks.

I shrug.

"She's nice, isn't she?"

The Rat smiles. Kind of sweetly actually. Then he changes the subject. He keeps doing that, filling up the silences.

"Are you having fun hanging out with Lake?" The Rat asks.

I know what the correct answer here is.

"Um, it's OK," I say.

He smiles again. This time like he's a bit relieved. As long as I say OK, then he is doing his job. I can tell that is what he's thinking.

"Oh, good," he says, kind of happy about it. "What do you girls do?"

"I dunno. Nothing," I say. "We went to a show at the Armenian Center."

"You went to a show?"

"Yeah," I say.

The Rat's impressed. Perhaps even hopeful.

"Was it fun?"

I shrug.

"How was the band?"

"I don't know."

"What were they called?"

"I don't remember."

"Did you like them?"

I shrug.

He gives up on his line of questioning because it is going nowhere. I can see he wants to push, but doesn't want to push too hard. I appreciate that. But I don't tell him that I do. I don't let on. I don't want to make it easy for him.

Why should I?

Nothing is easy for me. This whole summer, this whole being in Los Angeles thing is hard. Everything is hard.

Where's *my* bribe?

*　　*　　*

Later, when I am in the middle of a particularly juicy scene in the book I'm reading, the phone rings. The Rat doesn't seem to be picking it up, and maybe it's for me. Maybe it's Mom calling to tell me that she's changed her mind about staying in Peru. Maybe she's calling to tell me she's had enough of Peru and is coming home.

I run into the living room to pick up the phone.

The Rat is lying on the couch with his eyes closed and his earphones on, drumming on the air.

"Hello?"

"Hi, who's this?" a gravelly voice inquires.

"I'm Katy. Who's this?"

"I'm Frank. Is Beau there?"

"Yeah."

I walk over to The Rat and poke him. He removes an earphone and looks at me.

"It's Frank," I say, dropping the cordless on the couch next to him.

The Rat picks up the phone. I go to the kitchen, but I kind of take extra long, kind of hanging around as I eavesdrop on The Rat's side of the conversation.

"Hey, man, sorry I didn't make it tonight. . . . Nah . . . yeah . . . everything is OK. I'm doing fine. I know . . . I know . . . two weeks is a long time. It's my kid. She's here for the summer now, so the plan has changed and I don't think I'll make the Wednesday meetings for a while. . . . Yeah, I know . . . I think there's one in West Hollywood at seven a.m. I'll go Wednesdays before work. . . . Yeah . . . sorry I didn't check in with you. It was kind of last minute."

The Rat hangs up the phone and picks up a cigarette.

"Who's Frank?"

"He's my sponsor." He lights it up in the house and gives a big exhale. I don't make him go outside.

"I missed my NA meeting, my regular Wednesday night NA meeting. The one I've been going to every Wednesday for five years."

"Oh," I say.

And then I feel terrible. I know what the meetings are. I know that he should probably go.

"I'm old enough to stay at home at night," I say. "I know where the take-out menus are."

"Would that be all right?" The Rat smiles. " 'Cause I feel better when I go."

I shrug and nod. Then I go into my room and close the door. I don't want him to see how bad I really feel about him missing his meetings. I wouldn't want him to fall off the wagon because of me.

INSTITU-TIONALIZED

SUICIDAL TENDENCIES

Lake's room is painted all black, except for one wall, which is white with flyers and handbills and set lists and VIP stickers from shows pasted up like a thick wallpaper.

One of the VIP stickers is for the Red Hot Chili Peppers. It says ALL ACCESS. The date is 10/27.

"What's that?" I ask.

My mom has the same VIP pass in her shoebox at home.

"Patches," Lake says. "Homemade. I silk-screened them myself. My dad knows a guy who has a screen."

I meant the wall. I meant the shows. I meant the VIP pass. She knows it, too. But I guess she doesn't want to answer me. The wall speaks for itself. It's a rock shrine.

I know one thing. *She* wasn't at that show.

"Did Suck play that night?" I ask.

"That's where they met," Lake says.

"Who?"

"Our moms!" She throws her hand up and sort of indicates a painting hanging on the black wall next to the bed. I scoot over and look at it. It's a nude. It's a person's back, hint of a profile, from behind. Thick paint. Ripped up pieces of yellowed newspaper make up the body. The body is suspended in darkness. The hair. Oh. A Mohawk. It's a portrait of Sam Suck. In the lower right-hand corner, I see the signature. Yana Banana.

Let's be friends! Yana Banana.

"Did you know I got free classes at the Silverlake Conservatory of Music?" Lake says. "Because Flea was in love with my mom. Everyone was in love with my mom. *Everyone.*"

"Yana Banana?"

"You think it's a stupid name," she says.

I didn't say it. She said it. I *thought* it.

"It's no more stupid than Exene. Or Siouxsie Sioux. Or Janet Planet. Or Poly Styrene," she says.

Or Lake Suck, I think.

But I don't say it. I want to know more. I dig a little. I test it out. I want to know. How close were they?

As if reading my thoughts, Lake gets up and goes over to a wooden chest at the foot of her bed and opens it up. She pulls out all kinds of shiny, colorful, strange-looking vintage dresses and puts them carefully on the bed. She would never wear those kinds of clothes, but she handles them gently. As though they are treasures. She digs deeper into the chest and pulls out a few books until finally she finds the one she's looking for. She brings it to me and puts it in my hands.

"There you go," she says.

It's a sketchbook. I open it and start to flip through the pages and pages of sketches of my mom, The Rat, Sam, and a baby that I figure is probably Lake. Mostly it's drawings, but sometimes there are some photographs taped into the book, or diary entries. I stroke the page whenever I see a drawing of my mom. I notice that whenever she's drawn with The Rat, they are always touching each other.

"I think your mom broke my mom's heart when she left," Lake says.

I look up from the sketchbook.

"I think your mom left because my mom couldn't stay clean even after I was born. I think your mom didn't want that for you."

"I'm sorry," I say.

"Why?" Lake says. "You're lucky. You dodged a bullet."

My eye falls on a photograph of a beautiful woman with blond spiky hair, holding a baby in the air. The baby's mouth is wide open, screaming, maybe happy, maybe scared. Totally Lake.

"She left my dad when I was three because he was just a disaster. Everyone thought he'd be the one that ended up dead, not my mom."

Lake keeps talking like she's out of breath. Like she's running a marathon.

"All my life my mom would get clean, and then everything would be OK for a while. Then she'd mess up."

She doesn't even look up at me. She is telling me something about her mom, about her dead mom, while she is just cross-legged on the black shag carpet with a bunch of Grown-Ups patches surrounding her, like a moat.

"When I was nine, she was going to quit for real. She wanted to go and finish up and get her college degree. She was going to turn over a new leaf."

She is sewing or safety-pinning patches onto all of her jackets. While she talks, her hands keep busy.

"She had a lot of talent, you know. She probably could have been anything. She could have shown in galleries all over the world maybe. And now instead, she'll forever be nothing. She'll have forever never made it. She'll forever just be dead."

I should change the subject.

"Do you really make all your own patches?" I ask lamely.

Lake swallows twice, stops busying herself, and looks around like she sees a way out of having to cry. I feel relieved for both of us.

"Yep. I make all of my stuff myself. I make my own clothes. I peg my own jeans. I dye my own hair. I pin my own pins. Make my own lunch. I earn my own rips and holes. I like to keep it real, you know."

She likes to keep it real. And complicated.

"Do you want one on your jacket?" she asks, throwing me a patch. "It'd look good."

I put the sketchbook down and pick up the patch. I can't believe she's being serious. I nod.

I hand her my jacket, and she scrutinizes it until she nods in approval and starts to safety-pin the patch in the place she wants it. Then she hands me back the jacket and gives me a spool of thread.

I thread the needle and start sewing.

RUBY SOHO

RANCID

I am walking and Garth is half skating so I can keep up with him. I've got a few books in my bag from the library. I'm on the Ws. Wharton.

"Do you have to read those for school?" Garth asks. "Like a summer reading list?"

"No."

"You're reading them just for fun?"

"Yeah."

"You must have a huge brain," Garth says. "I don't read anything unless it's assigned or it's got pictures in it."

"OK," I say.

We pass by the wall with a mural of swirling black and orange graffiti all over it. People have written words all over the swirls. As we walk by it, Garth kisses his fingertips and then places his hand on the brick.

"Why'd you do that?"

"Do what?"

"Kiss the wall," I say.

"It's the Elliott Smith wall."

"The what?"

"Elliott Smith," he says, and he starts to sing.

"That's nice," I say.

"Yeah, he's pretty good," Garth says, getting kind of quiet. I can't tell if he's being super serious or shy. "I like sappy shoe-gazing boy sensitive stuff as much as I like punk. Don't tell anyone, though, because everyone already thinks I'm a pussy."

He is not kidding. He does seem all soft and skinny and girl-like.

"OK, I promise," I say. Anyway, I don't have anyone to tell.

"I know my secret inner sap is safe with you, Beige."

He might be safe with me, but in reality he's not safe at all. He wears everything right on his sleeve. He's got no filter. Maybe someone should tell him that he's thin-skinned. Maybe someone should tell him that if he wants to keep safe, he should keep quiet. Maybe someone should. But it isn't me.

"But I *love* punk, especially modern So. Cal. punk. See?" He flips his board to show me the stickers plastered underneath: NOFX, BLINK-182, GREEN DAY, THE TRANSPLANTS.

Is he saying that just to cover up? Is punk just a kind of armor to shield his soft heart?

I turn from him to look at the wall. I start reading the text. It's notes to Elliott Smith. Wishes for him.

It's a memorial.

"Is he dead?" I ask. "Is Elliott Smith dead?"

Garth looks surprised at my ignorance, but he's not mean about it.

"He stabbed himself in the heart. Or he was murdered. Case still open. He used to live around here. He played Sunset Junction once. I was too young to care. But I heard the show was legendary."

"Is everyone in this neighborhood a musician?"

"No," he says. "But I am. I'm going to be a great drummer like your dad."

"Is my dad that great?"

Garth clutches at his heart and flutters his eyelashes like he's having a heart attack or a seizure.

"Your dad is a *genius*. He does all these very complicated time measures that, like, no one else can do. They're impossible!"

"What is so great about drumming?"

"Don't you want to be a musician, Beige? You must have music in your blood."

"No way," I say. "Maybe it skips a generation."

There is a piano at Grand-maman's house. I have never once put my hands on the black and white ivory keys.

"Who plays?" I asked once.

"Moi et ta mère," Grand-maman said. "Your mother was very good, but she gave it up. It was for the best. Music made her too *passionate*."

Me, I never even wanted to start.

"I am a musical illiterate," I say.

But when Grand-maman sits down at Noël to play the standard Christmas carols, I always open my mouth and sing with her. My voice is just a high, shy, scratchy, whispery thing next to hers. I sing softly, as though I don't know the words, but I do.

"No, you're not," Garth says.

"I am, I swear." I indicate the wall with a wave of my hands. "I have never even heard of Elliott Smith."

"I bet you have."

"OK, *maybe*. But I don't know punk." There, I said it, and he didn't cringe.

"Sure you do."

"Name a band. I bet I haven't heard of them."

"Bad Religion."

"Nope."

"Dead Kennedys."

I shake my head no.

"Rancid."

"Is that the name of a band? Gross."

"Suck?"

"Um . . . maybe?"

Garth laughs, like belly laughs. Then he puts his arm around my shoulder, like he needs me to keep him standing up because he's going to fall down from laughing so hard.

"Oh, Beige, you are the funniest girl ever. Canada isn't that much in the Dark Ages. There are like fifty million amazing bands from there. Beige, admit it: you live under a rock, don't you?" he says.

My face feels hot. I shrug.

"I bet you have heard those bands and you don't even know it. I'm going to make you a mix CD, like a punk primer. I'll start with the basics. But I don't want you to take it the wrong way."

"Why would I take it the wrong way?"

"Well, because you know, it's a *mix CD*."

"So?"

"Well, I'm a boy and if I give you a mix CD, you know . . ."

I don't know. Why won't he just tell me?

"It's just a mix CD," I say.

"Yeah, exactly. But it would strictly be as friends, OK? Just to get you up to speed."

I don't really think I want a mix CD, but I don't want to hurt Garth's feelings. He's so into it. He starts naming bands and songs he thinks I'll like. And I just nod and go along with it. He can make me the mix CD. I don't have to listen to it. I can just say thank you.

"You know, a lot of cool bands were really influenced by Suck. I even have some covers of Suck songs that I'll throw on there."

He claps his hands and smiles at me.

I smile back. I smile to hide my loss for words.

My complete lack of awareness about all things music.

"I knew you'd understand," Garth says.

What it is it about music that captures the imagination of everyone I know? Why does everyone want to be a musician?

Music is dangerous. You could end up like Elliott Smith, stabbed right in the heart.

DAMAGED

BLACK FLAG

When I get home from hanging out with Garth, I find The Rat in the living room, shaking.

"I've had a really bad day, Katy," he says.

"OK," I say.

"Do you know what I want more than anything else in the world?"

I don't say anything because I know this is not the kind of question you answer. It's rhetorical.

"I want to get fucked up."

I am standing there like a statue. He turns and faces me. His face is wet with tears, from frustration or rage, or both. I don't know what to do. I don't know what's going on. I don't know how to help.

He clenches his fists. He punches the sides of his legs. It makes an irregular beat, which makes my heart break.

"Am I hungry? No. I ate. Am I angry?" The Rat looks over at me and shakes his head no. "Am I lonely? Tired?"

That's when he starts to shake more.

"Wait. I *am* angry. I am fucking pissed off. Stupid same shit. Stupid Sam. OK. You're angry at Sam, Beau. That's OK. You've been angry at Sam before, and you'll be angry at him again."

He rubs his hand on his head. He goes to the closet and disappears inside, to the safety of the drum kit, and bangs away, maniacally. I am still standing in the living room. I am sweating, and I want to take my sweater off, but I don't. I'm frozen in my position. I'm standing still as a statue in the living room, watching the closet door, and listening to him and the faint familiar thuds as he crashes his sticks on the cymbals.

I have never seen Mom do anything like this. Or has it been offscreen? Has Mom just gone into the bathroom and closed the door and drawn herself a bath? Has she just maybe made sure that I only ever saw her strong? I don't want to move because I want to ask someone a question, but I'm at a loss for words and there is no one to ask. All I can do is listen to The Rat drum the pain away.

He stops his drumming. He comes out of the closet. His sticks look sharp in his hands. He holds them like daggers. He looks at me. I am still standing in the same place.

"Every single day I wake up and I want to get fucked up. Every day. Every day I have to remind myself of the reasons why I don't want to. Every day I have to say, 'Today I'm not going to use (1) Because it's killing you. (2) Because your hands are steady when you drum now. (3) Because you got banned from Canada for it. (4) Because it took you away from your little girl.'"

His hands unclench from the sticks he was holding on to like weapons, and he lays them down on the coffee table. He takes a breath. He looks at me, with clear eyes. The wildness in them has receded. He smiles.

"It's OK. You know what they say, Katy? They say this: HALT. You most want to do drugs when you are Hungry, Angry, Lonely, or Tired."

He rubs his head. It looks like it needs a shave.

"I'm OK. It's going to be OK. Did I scare you?"

I nod.

"I'm sorry," he says. "I'll try not to let it happen again."

I finally take off my sweater and breathe. I sit down on the couch.

"Do you know how cool you are, Katy?"

"I'm not cool," I say. I tug on the holes in the knit blanket. It's like touching my mom. It makes me feel safe.

"You're cooler than I was at your age," The Rat says, joining me. "Your mother did a great job."

He leans over and squeezes my shoulder, or maybe he's trying to hug me.

"When I was fourteen, I was smoking dope and getting drunk," The Rat says. "I think your mom had run away twice by then. I gave myself my first tattoo when I was thirteen. See?"

The Rat flicks his wrist open to me and points to an ugly little skull and crossbones on his wrist. It is pathetically ugly compared to the other tattoos he has covering his arms.

"Why didn't you cover it up? It looks ugly next to the rest of them," I say.

"This one was my first. If your body is a map of your life, then I don't want to cover up where I came from. I've covered up other stupid ones I got. But that one, that one is special."

After falling into a lull for a while, I break the silence.

"I'm going to check my e-mail," I say.

I leave the living room. I don't want to hear about Mom with him and their wild ways right now. I don't want to be reminded of how different I am from them.

I want to make my own decisions. I want to do what I want. But I'm scared.

They didn't listen to anyone but themselves. But look where it led them.

ANARCH IN THE U.K.

THE SEX PISTOLS

Although she comes to hang out at my pool almost every day now, Lake won't get into the water. She doesn't swim, ever.

"I don't get wet," she says.

My skin is all pruney from staying in the pool for too long. I stayed in hoping that it would be just long enough for Leo to show himself. But there's been no sign of him. I pull myself out of the water and start to towel off.

Lake is following her usual routine, sitting in a lounge chair, fully dressed, with a big hat on so as to avoid the sun, scribbling lyrics into a composition notebook. Garth is still in the pool and he swims up to me and Lake, but he doesn't come out and join us. He hangs on to the edge. He is looking up at Lake, kind of gazing at her. Whenever he sees Lake, he is always trying to get her attention. I think I know why he is staying in the water so long. He probably doesn't want Lake to see his boner.

"I think I'm, like, a nihilist," Garth says.

This makes Lake look up from her notebook, kind of curious, but with a wary eye.

"A nihilist?" I ask.

"I believe that it is necessary to destroy the current political and social institutions to enable the future improvement of them."

"I know what nihilism means," Lake says.

Well, I didn't. I was glad for the definition. That's an interesting word.

"Yeah, like school needs to be destroyed," Garth says to me, but really it's for Lake's benefit. He's trying to impress her. He's so transparent. "School is an archaic institution."

"So why do you go then?" Lake says.

"My mom makes me," he says, and then shrugs. "My mom says I can be whatever I want once I'm eighteen, but as long as I live under her roof and eat her food, I have to be all talk and no action."

"I like school," I say. "I wouldn't want to destroy it."

"Why?" Lake asks.

I think about it.

"Books, knowledge, learning," I say. But as soon as I say it, I realize that I've been getting all those things at the Los Feliz Library.

"And socializing," I add. "Boys."

Lake shrugs. Meaning my answer is OK with her. At least it's honest.

Maybe I *don't* need school. But if I say that, then there will be a flaw in my saying that I like school. I'll have to take it back. And I don't want to. I *do* like school. I do like *going* to school.

"If he is a nihilist, why is he always wearing an anarchy T-shirt?" Lake says to me, like Garth isn't there, right in front of her, hanging on to her every word. Like she doesn't see him.

Now I shrug. Meaning I don't know. Don't ask me questions I can't answer.

"He should at least wear the right symbol," Lake says. "It's a nautical star or a backward *N*."

"Yeah, well, anarchists, nihilists, you know, they are both rebellious," Garth says. "They are both antiestablishment, and that's what I am." I can tell that he's a bit upset. He wanted to look and sound cool to Lake, and she's shot him down.

"And just FYI, if you were a real nihilist, you wouldn't listen to your mother," Lake says, laughing. "Mama's boy."

That must give her an idea, because she opens up her notebook again and scrawls something down. When she is done scribbling, she gets up.

"I'm outta here," Lake says. "I've got band work to do." She leaves.

Garth looks crushed. Like maybe he thinks I'm not so interesting, like the party is over now that Lake is gone.

"Want to make some sandwiches?" I say. "I'm kind of hungry."

He nods, so I hand him his towel so he can get out and not be embarrassed. He towels off and we walk up to the apartment.

Garth doesn't say anything. He heads straight for The Rat's drum kit and sits behind it. He takes out some sticks from his messenger bag and starts to air drum. He doesn't dare hit the skins.

Maybe it's just the chlorine, but his eyes are a bit red, like he's been crying.

He stops air drumming.

"I know that there is a difference between anarchy and nihilism," he says. "I just get them mixed up sometimes."

"It's an easy thing to do," I say. I don't tell him that I didn't even know that there was a difference.

"You could hit the skins," I say. "Go ahead."

"But they're The Rat's drums," he says. "I couldn't."

"The Rat says that pounding them makes him feel better."

"I say that, too!" Garth says.

"See?" I say. "So you know, he'd probably approve."

"You sure?" he asks.

"Go crazy."

Garth starts smashing on the skins and the cymbals and just letting it all out. Maybe it is better than crying. Maybe it's the same thing.

I think about that as I close the door to the soundproof closet and go into the kitchen and start making sandwiches. I put the yellow cheese slices on the bread to the beat.

LEXICON DEVIL
THE GERMS

Trixie's door is open when I get there. I can see
her through the screen dancing in the living
room. I watch her. She looks very focused. As her
body moves, it speaks in sentences. Womanly sentences. Her body writhes to a music I can't hear. It
must be music she carries inside of herself. Everyone else seems to do that around here — carry music inside of them like a secret.

Trixie does a twist, and her face lights up as she
spies me standing outside the door. She's not even
startled that I've been watching her; she just
smiles.

"Hi, Katy," she says. "I just had an idea for my
act. I'm trying it out. What do you think?"

I think she should maybe twist less. But if I said that, she'd ask me why and then I would have to come up with a reason and the only reason I have would be *because*. And I think she doesn't really care what I think. I think she just wants me to *care*.

So I just nod.

Trixie smiles and gives up. I kind of wish she wouldn't. I kind of wish she would have pressed me harder. Mom would have. I might have liked it if Trixie tried.

"Well, there are snacks in the fridge," she says.

I nod again.

Trixie nods.

"I thought I saw you and Lake with some girl at the pool the other day."

"Oh, well, yeah. He's a boy," I say.

Garthon stupide.

"You know, you can invite a friend over when you sit if you like," she says. "Even a boy."

She looks at me like she wants me to share some gossip with her.

"I don't have any friends here," I say.

I know she wants to bond with me. She bites

her lip and nods, like she's going to just let it go. But then I see her wince as she opens her mouth to speak.

"Katy," she says. "I'd like to be your friend."

"Because I'm The Rat's daughter," I say.

"Sure, that's one reason, but not only because of that. Because I like *you*," she says.

It would be nice to believe her.

"Growing up, I didn't know any girls like you. Girls who were funny and sweet and smart and kind," she says. "You're the kind of girl I always wished I was friends with when I was your age, so I am glad I get a chance to know you now."

I've noticed that most people hide things about themselves. Not Trixie. It's not just her mermaids and love for burlesque that are on display; it's everything, including her feelings and thoughts. I don't think I've ever met anyone quite like Trixie. I kind of admire that.

I guess I kind of like her, too. I don't have to automatically *love* her or anything just because she's The Rat's girlfriend.

"OK, I guess."

She smiles and then I wave good-bye as the

screen door shuts with a swish behind her as she leaves.

"There's a package for you," The Rat says when I get back to the Rat Hole. "I picked it up for you from the post office today."

It is sitting on the coffee table.

It's a brown-paper package, with lots of Peruvian stamps affixed to it. I go to my room for privacy. I don't want to open it up in front of The Rat. I sit on my bed and I take my time undoing the package.

Inside there is a hand-woven alpaca hat, a package of Peruvian hot chocolate, a large silver charm bracelet, and an Incan-looking statue. Even though it's hot, I put the hat on. I slip the bracelet on my wrist, and I put the statue on the table next to my bed.

I save the best for last. I reach in and pull out a postcard from Mom. On the front is a photo of Machu Picchu. I flip it over.

Home is where the heart is, it says. *And my heart is always with you. Je t'aime, Maman*

SHIT FROM AN OLD NOTEBOOK

THE MINUTEMEN

It's becoming a thing, Lake invading my bedroom. She is sitting on my bed reading *Paste* magazine while I am reading Leticia's new blog. I am filled with jealousy. I could write a blog, only it would be boring. It would be *beige*. Nothing exciting ever happens to me. If I wrote a blog, everyone back home would know how much my time in Los Angeles is just a big time stop and then they'll know that I'm in limbo. So I just post comments on their blogs to say I'm too busy to post anything about my life here.

But then I have to turn off my computer because Leticia e-mails me to say that I sure do comment a lot. Maybe I should comment less, so I look like I'm more busy. I'll be on cyber silence for a while.

The Rat knocks on the door.

"Yeah," I say.

"Garth just called—he's coming over," The Rat says through the closed door.

Lake rolls her eyes. I want to tell her to be nice. But I don't because she would probably laugh and use it against me if I told her not to hurt Garth's feelings.

I open the door in anticipation of Garth's arrival and see him walking down the hallway toward my bedroom. He starts to come into my room and then he sees Lake. He looks down at his feet.

"Hey, Garth," I say.

"Hey, Beige," he says.

"I see you got yourself a new T-shirt," Lake says, pointing at his chest.

"Yeah," he says, pulling at the collar. "Nautical star. Sign of the nihilist."

"You wouldn't even have known that if I hadn't told you," Lake says.

"There's nothing wrong with correcting a mistake when you've made one," Garth says. "It's *admirable*."

Garth opens his messenger bag and hands me a CD.

"What's this?" I ask.

"It's that mix CD I promised you," he says.

"Thanks," I say. I guess I'm happy about it. "Wanna come in and hang out?"

I make room for him to come in. I want him to join us.

He kind of takes a step forward, but then looks over at Lake and stops himself.

"No, I'm busy today. I got places to be. I'll check you later."

It surprises me because I know he doesn't really have anywhere to be. He just doesn't want to hang out with me and Lake. Even though I know he really admires her. Garth doesn't care what people might think. He just cares what she thinks.

"Good, I'm glad he's not sticking around," Lake says. "He's such a poseur."

But I remember the Sam Suck Manifesto. *I will go my own way.*

Garth is going his own way. He's no poseur.

I throw the CD on the night table and go back to the computer. I'm not interested. I won't comment on Leticia's blog. I'll just lurk. I'm addicted to knowing what's going on back home.

"What's that?" Lake asks, picking up the CD. "So, Garth made you a mix CD?"

"Yeah," I say.

"*Oooohhhhh*. Now I get it! He made you a *mix CD!*" she says. "You know what that means! He *loves* you!"

"No, he doesn't," I say.

"If a guy makes a girl a mix CD, he is in love with her."

I don't want Garth to love me. No. Not him. He's just a friend.

"No, he said he'd make me one because I don't know anything about music. It's a punk primer. He specifically said that it wouldn't mean anything."

"Oh," Lake says. "Well, then that's no fun. I can't laugh at you. You know, *I* could have made you a mix CD."

"Well, you didn't offer."

"Well, maybe I will make you one," she says. She's irritated now. She's been one-upped by Garth. He'd be pleased, so secretly I'm pleased for him.

She flips over the homemade mixed-media-collage cover art Garth has made and clucks.

"What?" I say.

"What nothing. It's a pretty good mix," Lake says. "He might not be completely clueless."

Score two for Garth.

I want the CD. I stretch my hand out for it. Now I'm ready for it.

She hands me the cover as she gets off the bed and heads into the living room with the disc in her hand. I follow her and watch as she puts on the CD, pulls out the headphones, and lets the music blast out loud in the living room. Lake begins to dance and sing along. I look down and read the name of the first song.

"Los Angeles"—X

The Rat comes out of the kitchen with Trixie and sees Lake dancing. He smiles.

Lake is just the kind of daughter that The Rat would want. A girl who can tell that this is Good Music. A girl who gets up and dances. My feet are not moving. Not even toe tapping. I sit down on the couch.

Trixie starts dancing with Auggie in her arms. The Rat kind of joins in, bopping around a little, looking like a weirdo. His movements are un-smooth and out of time for someone who keeps time for a living. Trixie and The Rat feed off each other's moves and start dancing a bit crazier when the next song comes on.

I look down at the list.

"Amoeba"—Adolescents

When that song is done, Trixie puts Auggie on the floor and takes The Rat in her arms. They slow down and kind of couple-dance. Auggie is moving around them on the floor. He's laughing and danc-ing like a little man. He's got pretty good moves for a two-year-old. He must take after his mom.

I've only heard of one or two of the bands, but some songs seem vaguely familiar, like maybe I heard them on the CBC late at night, or on a movie soundtrack or The Rat's living-room stereo or car radio. As the laughing and dancing around me gets louder again, I just feel more lost, more left out.

The Rat stretches his arms out, reaching for me, inviting me to join him in the dance. I smile and shake my head, so he goes back to dancing with Trixie and Auggie and Lake. There is a party in my living room, and even though I have an invitation, I still feel out of place.

Instead, I close my eyes. The bass thumps through me. I don't know where the next part is going to go. The music feels like it's going to go off a cliff. Why does it change there? Why does it stop there? Why do the drums go like that? I can't tell where the songs will go to next. I want them to go one way and they refuse. I can't trust the songs and where they lead me.

And the words. The words are too raw. They might make me crazy. They might take me places I don't want to go.

WE'VE GOT THE NEUTRON BOMB

THE WEIRDOS

Auggie has finally gone to sleep. It only took forever. I creep to the window to pull down the shade to make it darker in the room. That's when I notice him. Leo. He's in the pool. I creep out of Auggie's room quietly and go to the window in the living room.

I look around and notice a pair of opera glasses on one of the bookshelves. They're quite fancy, typical Trixie. *Lorgnettes,* she calls them. They are too fancy for my T-shirt and jean shorts. I don't care. I put them up to my eyes and swing my gaze over to the pool.

A leg pops into view.

It's Leo's leg. I have to adjust myself since the lorgnettes can't be adjusted. I step back to view the whole body. I stare at him in his swimming trunks. My chest feels tight. He is so beautiful. His muscles are smooth and hard and well defined. There he is in front of me, almost touchable and nearly naked.

I feel at home in this world of near silence, where all I can hear is Auggie sleeping in the next room and my steady breathing, which gets a little heavier as I watch Leo in the pool. I don't ask myself why I'm staring. I push aside the thought that it might be wrong. I know I like it. I know I want to.

Maybe I *am* a pervert.

I look over every inch of Leo's body. I have never really had the chance to inspect a boy's body so intensely before. I mean, I have stared at pictures of topless celebrities and models in magazines and online. I have seen plenty of pictures and movies that had men's naked chests or naked asses in them. I have been to the swimming pool and the park and seen boys in their shorts with their shirts off, and Leticia and I skip back and slow-advance some scenes from certain movies we've rented. But only when we were alone in the house and no one could walk in on us because it could've been embarrassing.

But this looking through lorgnettes at Leo live is different. Here in Trixie's apartment, I can look without anyone telling me not to. I can stare and take my time. I feel kind of quivery inside when I watch him.

I examine him closely. I decide that I like Leo's sideburns but I'm glad he doesn't have hair on his chest.

Should I feel bad about spying on him?

I am about to put the lorgnettes down when someone else comes into view. Lake. What is she up to?

Leo is busy in the pool doing laps. Then he notices her. He has a grin on his face. No, it's more like a leer. He swims over to her. Now Lake is talking to Leo. I swing my view over to Lake. She is talking and gesticulating wildly. I crack open the window a little bit, but I can't hear what she's saying to him. Leo says something. Then he grabs her leg and tries to pull her into the pool.

Lake goes ballistic.

Lake takes his clothes and his towel and dumps them into the pool. Then she flips him the finger.

Leo is now all red and angry.

Lake heads out of the pool area. I know where she's heading: up to visit me. I put the lorgnettes back on the shelf and grab a book on Bettie Page and dive for the couch. I try to look as casual as possible.

She knocks on the door.

"What?" I say.

"It's Lake."

"Door's open," I say.

Lake comes in and plops herself down on the couch next to me.

"What are you looking at?" she asks. The page is open to a photo of Bettie and another lady posed in a bondage scene. "Perv."

I blush. I *am* a perv, but for totally different reasons.

"Shh, Auggie will wake up," I say, even though we are not being loud. "What's that?"

She is holding Leo's T-shirt in her hand.

"Oh, yeah. Shit," she says, laughing and flopping

over onto the cushion. "I guess I stole Leo's shirt. It's cool. It's from Threadless. Here, take it."

She hands me the T-shirt as she gets up and heads for the bathroom.

I can't help it. I lift the T-shirt and put it to my nose and inhale. It smells really good, musky and sweaty mixed up with the smell of outside fresh air and deodorant and chlorine.

"What are you doing?" Lake says to me. She's standing in the hallway. She's staring at me. I'm caught.

"Smelling."

"Oh." She cocks her head to the side, and I put the T-shirt back into her hands. She holds Leo's shirt up to her nose and drinks it in. "Yeah. Leo smells good."

"I wonder if I smell good," I say.

"I don't know. I never smell you," Lake says. "What about me? Do I smell?"

"You always smell like vanilla," I say. And BO but I don't say that.

"Oh yeah, I guess I do."

We hear someone yelling outside. Someone is screaming Lake's name. Leo.

"Oh, shit." Lake laughs. "He's pissed."

Lake takes the T-shirt and runs onto the balcony. I walk out after her just in time to see her throw the T-shirt off the balcony. It floats delicately to the ground. Leo scrambles for it as it lands. Then he looks up at us and gives us both the finger.

THE CREW
7 SECONDS

"This is it," Sam says.

The band is sitting in the living room, making plans. Big plans. Big comeback plans.

I sip lemonade, homemade. I made it with lemons from a tree in the courtyard. I put the glasses on a tray. I serve it to the band members, who take it greedily. They all have hope in their eyes. The air in the living room is exciting. Infectious. I catch it. I feel excited. Suck is getting back together for real.

"We can't fuck it up," The Rat says. He's grinning ear to ear.

"Yeah," Sam says. "We're back. Sunset Junction."

Lake crosses her fingers and holds them up in mock excitement.

Then she rolls her eyes at me. As excited as they are, I bet the conversation is boring to her because it's not about *her* takeover of the rock world. And I know her favorite subject is herself.

Lake thumbs for me to follow her. I do. We make our escape and head down to the courtyard, and then to the street in search of a free outside table at one of the cafés on Sunset.

"What?" I say.

"I haven't seen my dad this excited in years," she says. "This is a really good thing."

"Looks like it," I say.

"You don't even know," she says.

I am so tired of not even knowing.

"If all goes according to *my* master plan, the Grown-Ups is going to be the opening band on one of the stages at Sunset Junction."

"OK," I say. *So what?* I think.

"You need to be my roadie. And I need you to do merch."

"I'm not even in the band," I say.

"I told you the other girls aren't serious." She looks at me. "Besides, I trust you."

She's dead serious. I'm the one Lake trusts. That is weird.

"Yeah, OK," I say. "I'll help."

My eyes spy something more interesting over Lake's shoulder. On the street, coming toward us, is the Walking Man. Today he has his radio glued to his ear. Every day since I've been in Los Angeles, I see this guy walking around the neighborhood.

"Are you even listening to me?" Lake asks.

I ignore her and I wave to the Walking Man.

He doesn't even look up. He just adjusts his trajectory to weave around me. He just keeps walking.

"Why did you wave to him?" Lake asks.

"I see him every day."

"He's never going to wave back," Lake says. "The Walking Man doesn't acknowledge anyone who doesn't live in the neighborhood."

"Why is he always walking?" I ask.

"Nobody knows. Forget about him—he's in his own little world. Let's focus on the Grown-Ups."

We grab a seat at a café and order organic juices.

"It's at Skooby's Hot Dogs," she says.

"A hot dog stand?" I ask.

"It's not a hot dog stand like you think. Everything about them is totally rock. They have live rock shows on Saturday nights next door under an old marquee on Hollywood Boulevard. The best thing about it is that it's all ages. And that's what's important. I mean, it's hard to get shows when you're underage. My goal after Skooby's and Sunset Junction is that the Echoplex will let me open for someone really cool."

I get distracted from listening to her again. Leo is coming toward us with his posse in tow.

I sit up straight. I smile.

If I could just talk to him once, I know he would want to be my friend. I could explain about the T-shirt thing. It wasn't me. I bet he knows that I had nothing to do with it. We could laugh about it maybe, have a moment of mutual understanding. We could exchange a knowing look. Maybe say something like, *Oh, that Lake.*

"Hey," I say.

"Hey," he says back. Then he glares at Lake, who gives him the finger.

"God, Beige, are you even listening to me?" Lake says.

"What?" I ask.

"Are you going to help me out or not?"

"OK, fine," I say. "I'll help."

LOVE BUZZ

NIRVANA

Trixie's apartment is still. I peek in and look at Auggie, breathing deeply in his bed. His mermaid nightlight casts a low glow in his room.

I turn the TV on and realize that Trixie has no cable. Neither does The Rat. They are like weird peas in a pod. No wonder they are dating. They're kind of made for each other. I flip through the DVDs. Trixie has nothing I've ever heard of, or if I have, it's nothing I'd want to see. I find one on the burlesque scene from the turn of the last century. I pop it on.

Women on stage, heavy, dancing. The music is low. The moves luscious. I get up and feel my heart beating. I feel my knees moving. I grind and sway. I close my eyes. It's me and my feet. My hips. Moving. It makes me feel buzzy inside.

I imagine I am on that stage with them. I imagine the audience watching me. I imagine Leo watching me.

Leo.

A noise is coming from somewhere else, not the TV. I open my eyes. My moment of abandon and swaying by myself is gone. The women in black and white on the screen are still moving. They're at one with their bodies and the music.

What is that noise? I ask myself. Oh. It's yelling. Bloodcurdling screaming. It's a fight. A fight right next door. I try to hear the words. Can't understand any of the words. It's all in Spanish. The arguing stops suddenly with the slam of a door.

I turn down the volume with the remote. I walk to the balcony and step outside. Leo sits on his balcony. He looks up. Doesn't say a word. Just nods. Then he rests his head in his hands.

Leo's not looking at me. We are just sitting, outside, each on our own balcony, and all I can think of is how there is such a tiny space between us.

I try to quiet my heart, which is pounding loud in my chest.

I want to turn to him and say something. If I could just think of something smart to say. This could be my moment. Like in the book I'm reading. I'm at the *T*s. Tolstoy. *Anna Karenina*. He could be my Vronsky. I don't think about the fact that I don't think that story is going to end well.

This is my moment. I imagine I open my mouth and tell him my truth. Something like: *"Sometimes my feelings get so big that I just want to swim out into the darkness. Just jump off the end of the world. Sometimes I want to dig, right down to the bones of everything,"* I say. *"My mom digs. She digs in the earth. Right into the past. She says that sometimes when you dig, you dig up stuff you might not want to find. But that's where the good stuff lies."*

Then I can picture him moving his hand out between the grate of the balcony and grabbing mine. He'd look into my eyes.

I can just imagine it.

Suddenly, I realize Leo is looking at me. For real. Those eyes. In the world, there are only those eyes.

"You here just for the summer?"

"Yeah."

"Your dad is The Rat."

"Yeah."

This is it. This is it.

"You friends with Lake?"

I nod. OK. It's still going well.

"Leonardo! Leonardo entra la casa ahora mismo!"

"You like parties?" he asks.

I nod.

"There's one tomorrow night at my friend's house on Benton, just off Sunset."

"Leonardo!" his mother is screaming.

"I'll be there at eight. You should come. You and Lake should both come."

Then he laughs.

"OK, thanks," I say.

He asked me out.

Well, not really. But it's kind of like he asked me out.

"See you there." He nods and gets up and heads to the door.

And then he disappears inside.

I think he takes my heart with him.

SIX PACK GIRL
NOFX

I call Lake.

"What do you want?"

"There is a party tonight," I say.

"Yeah, so?"

"We should go."

"I don't do parties."

"I don't want to go by myself," I say.

"Why don't you ask your girlfriend Garth?"

"Leo invited me," I say. "I don't want him to think I'm on a date with Garth."

Lake is quiet for a minute.

"He said to invite you, too." I don't tell her that he was laughing when he said it. I don't want her to laugh or tell me I'm stupid.

"Where is it?" she asks.

"On Benton," I say. "Off Sunset."

"Oh, God, that's Marco's house," Lake says. "He's such a player."

"Maybe you could hand out flyers there for your Skooby's show," I offer.

"OK," she says. "I'll go. But it's strictly business."

When Lake comes over to pick me up, her black eyeliner is smeared more than usual and that's when I realize that she's probably been crying.

"What's wrong?" I ask.

"Like you'd care," she says.

I might care if she tried me. I don't say anything. I have learned that if I wait long enough, eventually she'll cough up what's on her mind.

I lock the door behind me and follow quietly behind Lake. Her body in motion looks like it's an attack on the air and an assault to the pavement. It's like she wants to fight with everything.

"The only reason I'm coming is because those bitches bailed on me for practice tonight." It's always about the band. Always how the band is holding her back.

At the party, Lake doesn't say hello to anyone until she finds the beer. I stay out of her way. She can just cool off. She brings me a beer but I don't accept it. I don't drink.

"Fine, more for me, then," she says.

I go and find a soda and then start scanning the room for Leo. He said he'd be there at eight p.m. By nine-thirty, I'm still standing in the corner with Lake. I'm feeling bored and I'm staring at the door, willing it to open and for Leo to finally step through it. Only when Leo arrives will the party really start.

I scan the room. People are huddled in corners. Music is blasting. Some kids are making out. There's black light making everything glow. I notice a girl stumble out of the kitchen. She's laughing hysterically as she trips over someone's legs and stumbles.

This is not my kind of party. I ignore the crazy and concentrate on the door.

Lake goes on and on, providing me with a nonstop color commentary on how boring and lame everyone at the party is. Everyone is a poseur. Everyone has betrayed her. Everyone has a problem. She's such a victim. Fuck them all. Blah, blah, blah.

I wonder if it ever crossed her mind that she's the one with the social problem.

I tune her out and think of Leo.

Time keeps ticking by. He said to meet him here.

Where is he?

And then Leo walks in. Everything starts to move in slow motion and everyone around him blurs out. It is only him. Time stops.

"Oh, look what the cat finally dragged in," Lake says.

Leo is with a posse of friends. He stands in the doorway and surveys the room. He looks gorgeous. His hair is perfectly tousled. He's wearing khakis just like me, and flip-flops and a blue and white button-down shirt. The top two buttons are open, and I can see the hollow at the base of his throat. And his smooth skin.

Who am I kidding? A guy like Leo isn't going to notice a girl like me.

He's obviously going to pass me by. So many girls go right up to him and say hello. They surround him.

He could have his pick of anyone. Maybe he just asked me here to be nice. To be neighborly.

But it's me who he walks right up to.

"Hey, Katy, you made it," he says. He calls me Katy. Not Beige. *Katy*.

He ignores Lake.

"Yeah," I say.

"Cool," he says. Then he leans up against me. He puts one arm on the wall behind me, kind of pinning me in, and with the other hand he traces my cheek and then he leans his face into mine and kisses me.

I am kissing. At a party. I am kissing a god at a party. He's moving his hands up and down my arms. I feel all shivery.

"See ya," I think I hear Lake say next to me. I don't know. I'm too busy kissing.

When he breaks away from me, I catch my breath. I notice Lake is gone. I don't care.

"You're a good kisser," he says, and then kisses me again. And I don't tell him that I've never kissed anyone before. I just go with it.

He licks my neck. He sucks on my neck. He sticks his tongue in my ear. I do whatever he does right back to him. I even feel up his chest.

He bites my earlobe and then whispers, "Do you want a beer?"

Even though I don't want one, I say, "Yeah."

I don't tell him that I don't drink beer. I don't want to seem uncool.

He disappears into the kitchen to get us beer and brings them back and I just drink it. And then I kiss him some more.

"Oh, I love this song," he says, and he puts his mouth next to my ear and begins singing in a whisper to me. And for the first time I really hear the music that is playing, and I feel how it accents the moment. Heightens it. I don't say I don't know who the band is or what song it is.

I just agree.

I just say, "Me, too."

CRASH!

Sounds of bottles falling and someone thudding and people laughing. And then I hear it.

"You bitches blew off practice!"

I turn around, breaking away from Leo, to see Lake is shouting at the girls from her band. They look together and collected, like they just stepped out of a magazine photo shoot. Lake looks like a mess.

They are laughing at her.

"We have to stick together!" Lake is yelling at them with her high-pitched baby voice.

"Why?" one of the girls—I think her name is Zoe—says.

"Because we're a *band*. A band is like blood. We're a team," Lake yells, pushing the hair back that keeps falling in her face. I have a ponytail holder in my bag she could borrow, but I just stand back and watch the fireworks. I don't want to get my head cut off when I am trying to help.

"The point is," Lake says, "if we're going to make it, we have to practice."

"But, why do we have to practice so *much*?" Zoe asks.

"Because, duh, that's the only way to get better," Lake says. "I practice every single day."

"Which is why you're not really socialized," one of the girls—Kim, I think—says.

"Look, we don't have to be best friends," Lake says. "We just have to be great together."

She kind of stumbles as she leans forward to make her point, and the keg cup goes flying out of her hand and rolls across the floor, spilling all its beer.

A bunch of people laugh, and for a second, I kind of feel bad for her.

"That bitch needs to be housebroken," one of the girls says, and then high-fives one of the other girls.

Then Lake's fist comes flying out, but before it connects, one of the boys has pinned her arms behind her back.

"Fuck off!" she shouts, trying to shake the boy off her. The Skooby's flyers she brought flutter to the floor.

There's more laughing.

I should really do something, but Leo pulls my face back toward him.

"Forget about her," he says. Then he sticks his tongue in my mouth. I have no choice; I can't say anything. I just keep kissing.

Later on, one of Leo's friends comes over and interrupts us.

"Yo, Marco," Leo says. "What's up?"

Marco looks at me. "You're Lake's friend, right?"

"Not really," I say. I don't know why I say that except that I know Leo doesn't think Lake is cool.

"Well, you came here with her, right?"

I nod.

"She's puking her guts up in my bathroom. Can you get her out of here?"

At first I don't move. But Leo and Marco are just kind of looking at me.

"It's OK," Leo says. "You should probably go help her."

So, even though I don't want to, I follow Marco down the hallway to the bathroom.

Lake is lying on the floor, her arms draped around the toilet bowl, her hair covering her face. Her dirty black sweatshirt is covered with Grown-Ups patches, meticulously hand sewn. This is no Hot Topic outfit. Lake even looks like she's keeping it real when hugging a toilet.

She retches again. I try to hold her hair back, but there's too much of it. I take the ponytail holder out of my hair and wrap it around hers.

Lake looks up at me. One eye open, trying to focus. I bet she's seeing double.

"Can you just get me out of here?" she slurs. "Beige, *please* just get me out of here!"

There is a little piece of vomit in the corner of her mouth. I take a piece of toilet paper and wipe it off. I can't leave Lake. I don't want to take her home. But I pick her up off the floor and lead her out of the house. I want to say good-bye to Leo, but I don't see him.

What should I do? Think, Katy, think. Whatever you do, just don't make a beige choice. Get it right. It wouldn't be good for her grandmother to see her all messed up.

I know. I'll take her to her jam space. It's not so far from here. I can think about what to do there.

I go through all of Lake's keys and try to find the one that opens the door.

Lake, knowing where she is, stumbles out of my arms and gropes for the angel, producing a spare key from behind its wing.

"There," she says, holding up the key. She stumbles to the door and tries to put it in the lock, but gives up and so I do it.

When the door finally opens, she pushes past me and flops down onto the couch.

I pop open the fridge and get her a Coke.

"Drink this," I say.

I want to go back to the party. I don't want to be here. Maybe I can leave her now. Maybe I've done enough. I will still win my nice-girl points.

"Get me a blanket," Lake demands.

I look around. I shrug.

Can't I just go?

Lake starts waving madly, so I turn and I notice a wardrobe. I open it up and find a bunch of jackets, and at the bottom, there is a sleeping bag. I pull it out. Underneath it, I notice a knit blanket. I know that knit.

I cover Lake with the sleeping bag and sit at her feet, and I wrap myself in the knit blanket. My mom's knit blanket. It's probably the one she sent to Sam Suck, or to Yana.

Lake starts monologuing, but it makes no sense at all. I can only understand, like, every fifth word, and the thread of her thoughts is all over the place. She's mixing up school, band, the world, unfairness, Leo, me, Sam Suck, people, making out, sex, love, and rock and roll.

She's just messed up. She's just drunk. She's not in control of herself. I don't like it. It scares me.

I'm a little buzzed, but I don't know if it's from the half beer I drank or from kissing Leo.

"Lake, are you ever afraid?" I say, pulling the blanket tighter around me. She probably won't answer me. She probably can't focus on what I'm saying. But it feels good to ask her something from my heart right out loud.

"Afraid of what?" Lake mumbles after a minute, surprising me.

"That we'll become addicts," I'm whispering. "That we'll lose control?"

"No," Lake says. "I'm not going down that road. No way."

"I'm afraid of it," I say.

I don't say anything after that.

I am quiet for a while. I'm not going to go back to the party.

"Your hair looks really good like that," Lake says. "You should wear it down more often."

The next sound I hear is her snoring.

I flip open my cell phone and call The Rat.

While I'm waiting for him to get there, I walk around the jam space. I'm feeling too hopped-up on endorphins or adrenaline or kissing or beer or truth to sit still. And the space, walking this jam space, is soothing. That's when I see it, handwritten words on the wall. I thought it was graffiti or something, but it's not. It's something more than that. It's hard to see from anywhere but up close that the handwritten words are sentences. I move some of the instruments aside so I can get close and read what's written.

My name is Lake Suck and this is my manifesto. I swear to be myself. To think for myself. I will not be led by social conventions. I will make my own way through the world. I will live on my own terms without conforming to society's expectations of who they think I should be. I will be the visible minority.

By being myself, I will help to save the world. I swear to always look, listen, learn, think, ask, act, and speak for myself.

The Rat knocks on the jam space door and it makes me jump. Like I've been caught with my thoughts hanging out. Caught agreeing. He knocks again. I forgot I locked the door behind me because I was scared. I let him in.

"Whoa," he says. "This is twice as big as mine."

He looks around, nodding in approval. I wonder if it feels as good to him in here as it does to me.

"Is she OK?" he asks.

"I think so. She got drunk. She fought with her friends."

"OK, we'll call Mrs. Hassock and let her know that Lake is all right."

"It's not too late?"

"Mrs. Hassock's rules. When we were growing up, as long as Sam and I called his mom to tell her where we were sleeping, no matter what time, she didn't care where we were."

"What about you?" I ask. "What about your parents?"

The Rat shakes his head.

"They didn't care," The Rat says. "I pretty much lived at the Hassocks'."

The Rat came out in the middle of the night and picked me up.

He didn't mind at all. He was fine about it. He was glad I called.

No questions asked.

OH BONDAGE, UP YOURS!

X-RAY SPEX

Lake leans too long on the doorbell. I know it's her, and I don't want to answer. She doesn't give up, and I know she won't go away.

I don't want to talk to her.

But then she starts screaming my name up at the window, so I break down and I let her in.

She blows into my room like nothing happened last night and shoves a shirt into my hand.

"This is for you," she says. "I don't wear it anymore."

It's a faded black T-shirt with a maple leaf on it. It says CANADUH.

I take it as her way of saying thank you. Or I'm sorry. She should be sorry! She's supposed to say it. I deserve an apology. I don't even know why I took care of her.

But she'd never say the words. She's not that kind of person. It bugs me. No one is that kind of person. Except me. I could be. I am. I say it. I say the words.

"I'm sorry about what happened," I say.

"That's cool," Lake says. "No problem."

She doesn't get it. I wasn't asking for her forgiveness. I was saying it as a hint, for her to follow my lead for once. I was saying it like, *I'm sorry you were drunk, that sucks for you. You must be so embarrassed. I would be.*

Now I'm mad. I want to explode.

I am standing in the middle of my room trembling as I watch Lake sit on my bed as per usual with my guitar. She looks up at me.

"Fuck it. I said I'm over it," she says, leaning toward me. As though she's being earnest.

Doesn't she know I wiped puke off her face? Held her hair back? Gave her a soda? Let her lean on me because she could hardly walk?

"I'm totally hungover," she says. "But I've got to jam. Wanna come?"

"No," I say. I start swallowing a lot. I'm burning up.

"What's up?" she says. "You look weird."

Great. She's finally noticing something besides herself.

If she were my real friend, then she would have known. Or seen. Or remembered.

I just wanted to be with Leo. I didn't want to take care of her.

If she were a real friend, I could tell her. Tell her about Leo and me. It would be nice to talk with someone, because I feel confused. If she were a real friend like Leticia, I could talk to her about it.

If she were a real friend, I could ask her, what does it mean when you make out with a guy all night at a party? Does it mean something?

"Speak," Lake says.

But I don't want to share this feeling with her. She'll drown it.

I squeeze my eyes shut. I don't want to cry.

"Beige. *What* is up?" she asks.

I don't say anything.

"OK! OK! I know! I'm a dick. I got drunk. I made a scene! I'm *sorry*," Lake says.

She means it. She is sorry. She said it.

It doesn't make me feel better.

"Did I do something? Did I puke on you?" she asks.

"No."

"Well then, what?" she says. "I didn't fight with you, right? I fought with the Grown-Ups."

"I was hanging out with Leo," I say finally. "But then I had to stop and take care of *you*."

"This is about Leo?" Lake asks.

"No," I say.

Yes, it is. It is about Leo. And how I'm *not your friend*. I want to say it. I could say it. But I don't. Because she is like my not-friend. Like Los Angeles is my not-home. And the nice girl inside of me can't be too mean.

"You didn't have to do that. Take care of me," Lake says. "I can handle myself. I'm *housebroken*."

I count to ten before I speak. I try to calm myself down.

"Who else was going to do it, Lake? You had your head down a toilet. You hate your band. You're a bitch to everyone. You have no friends. *Everybody* needs friends."

My voice is getting louder and higher. I hear the pitch changing as I get more breathless. I sound crazy to my own ears.

I can't believe I said it, but it's true, I think. Even I need a friend, which is why I've tolerated Lake all summer.

"I *have* friends. They're just not in high school. They're musicians. Real ones," Lake says. "And I have you. You're my friend."

"I'm not your friend for real. We're temporary," I say. "And now Leo thinks I'm lame because he thinks I'm your friend."

"Oh," Lake says. "I see."

"Oh?"

Lake just sits on the bed. She kind of looks at the black nail polish on her fingers. She kind of looks off out the window.

"Let me tell you something about Leo, as your *temporary* friend. He's a player. He's a jerk. And he's an asshole."

"How would you know?" I ask.

But I know how she knows. I saw them by the pool, through the lorgnettes, fighting like they were more than friends.

"You have something going on with Leo, don't you?" I ask.

"I did," Lake says. "It's ancient history."

"Why didn't you tell me?"

"Because I don't like him," she says. "I needed to get material for my songs. I can't write about nothing."

"What does that mean?"

"I just needed him for the angst," she says. She seems flustered.

"You used him?"

"Yes. I mean, no. It was *fun*. But he's not, like, ever going to be the love of my life. He's not a kindred spirit or anything. He's not even my *type*."

"You're a user," I say. "You use people."

"I just haven't met my tribe yet," Lake says.

"What?" I say. It sounds like something I might think.

"Do you know how frustrating it is to be, like, a twenty-six-year-old trapped inside a sixteen-year-old body? I can't do anything that I want to do. I can't do anything that I'm ready for. I have to wait and get this whole teenage thing out of the way before I can go and do what I want. I figure I might as well find *something* to write about," Lake says. "So yeah, I had a thing with Leo during the school year. Big deal. I just needed him for the angst. For my *songwriting*. And then he got all attached. And when I started hanging out with you, he tried to make me jealous by putting the moves on you."

She's wrong. She must be wrong. He likes me. He said so. I can't believe that he looked at me with those eyes and said those things and kissed me like that just to get back at Lake.

"That doesn't even make any sense. It wouldn't work. You would never be jealous of me, because I'm *beige*," I say.

"You know, you have a lot of angst," Lake says. "I bet you'd write great lyrics. You should maybe try it. Jot stuff down, get some of that rage out of you."

"I don't think so," I say. "I'm not the angry person. You are."

Lake starts laughing. Really laughing.

"Right, Beige, you're not repressing anything," Lake says. "Sure you don't want to write a song now?"

I shoot her a look.

I don't want to hear her lies about Leo anymore. I want to giggle with someone over him. I want to be excited. She doesn't know anything about anything. She wasn't there. She wasn't in his arms. He wasn't whispering in her ear. He likes me. For me. Not Lake.

"For what it's worth, I told him to stay away from you," she says.

I turn away from her.

She sighs big.

"OK, then, he's not an asshole. He really does like you. Don't believe me. Whatever. Maybe he is your true love. But I'll bet you one of my Guitar Center gift certificates that you don't hear from him anytime soon. It was a party. He used you. That's it."

"It's not like that," I say.

But deep down, I know it is.

"Maybe you're just jealous that I met a boy who really likes me."

Lake rolls her eyes.

"Come on, Beige. Let's go kick out some jams," she says.

"No," I say. "I'm going to stay here."

"The jam space makes everybody feel better," Lake says.

"So does the sun," I say. "But ultimately, it gives you cancer."

"HA! Those would make good lyrics," Lake says. "Actually, I'm going to write that down!"

She pulls out her notebook and scratches down what I said. Then she sticks her hands out for me to pull her up. I ignore her.

"You coming?" she asks.

"No," I say.

"Suit yourself," she says, and then she gets up and blows out of my room.

I wonder, though, what I would write down. I think about how I am feeling. Hurt. Hopeful. Giddy. Sad. Happy. Lonely. Frustrated. Betrayed. Girlie. In love. Dumb.

CHERRY BOMB

THE RUNAWAYS

I see him the next morning, in the pool, doing his laps earlier than usual. My heart jumps. I rush to get dressed. I put some lip gloss on. I pinch my cheeks. I check myself out in the mirror. I look pretty good.

I go down to the pool to meet him.

"Hello," I say. I say it like a heroine. I say it like a leading lady. I say it like his true love.

He looks away from me and adjusts his goggles.

I start to tremble. Maybe Lake isn't a liar. No. She can't be right.

"Leo," I say, more insistent. More desperate. I can't help it. I don't want Lake's version to be the truth. I reach my hand out to touch him. He moves away.

"Why are you ignoring me?" I ask.

He takes three long steps and dives back into the pool.

I stand at the edge and watch him do his laps.

It's not that I don't want to leave. I'm just stunned. Stunned into staying in place. I'm still standing there when Leo finishes his set and pulls himself out of the pool. He takes his towel and dabs his eyes, then dries himself off.

He has to pass me to get out of the pool area. He walks toward me. I won't let him through.

"What's going on?" I say.

I thought you liked me, I think. *All those things you said while we were kissing. Doesn't that mean anything to you? There must be something I can do or say that will make you be like you were at the party.*

He stops. Shakes his head.

"Just because we hooked up at the party doesn't mean I *like* you," he says.

He pushes by me and I offer no resistance.

My heart feels heavy, like it's being pulled under. I feel like I'm drowning.

I shudder. Then I start to cry.

WE GOT THE BEAT

THE GO-GO'S

"I knew you'd eventually find your way here," Lake says. She is on the floor of the jam space with the paper cutter, slicing Grown-Ups handbills into fourths. "Move that merch stuff and help me."

Why does she have to be right? Why does she have to know that I'd make my way here and that it does make me feel better?

"Why do you have all this merch?" I ask, moving one of the boxes to join Lake on the floor.

"That's how we're going to make money for my demo."

"Wouldn't it just be easier to ask your dad to pay for it?"

"Merch is also about creating a buzz, getting our name out there," Lake says. "You don't get it."

No. I don't. I don't get it. I still don't get it. It's like the millionth thing I don't get. What I should get by now is to just keep my mouth shut. I fall back to doing what I know how to do best, being quiet. It's easier. I stop what I'm doing and go sit on the couch and start reading.

"Excuse me. Weren't you, like, helping me?" Lake says.

"Now I'm reading."

"The other Grown-Ups girls were supposed to get here like an hour ago," Lake says. "I don't think they are coming."

How is this my problem? Why do I have to pick up their slack?

"Why do you play with them? You don't even like them. They're not even helpful."

"I had to get a new band after I kicked everyone out of my old band," Lake says. "At least this time they know how to play their instruments."

Lake seems to kick a lot of people out of her life. I wonder if she's planning on kicking me out. I bet she won't bother. She just thinks of me as a sidekick. No one kicks a sidekick out of their life. It's not even worth the trouble.

I submit to my fate, slide off the couch, and pull a stack of the handbills toward me. I start cutting them into fourths. Now that I've taken over, Lake dusts herself off and picks up her guitar, plugs in, and starts noodling.

Under her breath, Lake sings the same lyrics over and over again:

> *"My tiny heart*
> *Swims up to you*
> *And breaks apart*
> *Before anything even starts*
> *I still haven't heard from you.*
> *You turn*
> *Into nothing new."*

The lyrics kind of sneak into my head. It's how I feel about Leo. But not quite.

"Shit!" Lake says. Even though I'm used to her outbursts now, she startles me and I slip with the cutter. I draw blood. I suck on my finger. I don't complain. But I shoot her a look.

I stop cutting handbills. I'm thinking. There is no harm in asking her what the problem is. At least talking to her about her problem would distract me from thinking about Leo. It hurts to think about him.

"What's the problem?" I ask.

"The thing is about music is that there are only so many combinations. Or maybe it's that I only know a certain number of those combinations," Lake says. "This one sounds a little like the Go-Go's song 'We Got the Beat.'"

She starts to play.

"Listen to it. Tell me. Am I wrong? We got the A, we got the D, we got the G, C, we got the A!" I watch her fingers as she presses on the strings. Her fingers fly. They press; they speak in code.

We got the A, we got the D, we got the G, C, we got the A!

I repeat it in my head as she repeats it on the guitar. Then she starts to play her new song.

"What do you think? Too similar?" she asks.

"Maybe you need to work on the way you sing it? Maybe emphasize something different?"

She shrugs.

"Duh!" she says. "But what?"

I shrug back. "I don't know!"

"Yeah." She laughs. "You don't."

Then Lake starts futzing around with the song again.

She sings it a million more times. She plays it in a million more different ways. But suddenly, to my ears, the solution is obvious. It's not the music that's wrong; it's the words. The words aren't right. I scribble something down on the back of one of the flyers.

"Lake," I say.

She looks up from the guitar.

"What?"

I say her lines back to her, with a twist:

> *"It's been*
> *three days*
> *still haven't*
> *heard from you.*
>
> *My heart*
> *lives underwater*
> *breathing for you.*

But you
break apart
my tiny heart,
giving me
no chance to start
something
with you.

I dove into the pool
I dove in
hoping to swim
now I'm drowning."

"Hey, I like that, Beige. It's kind of poetic."

When she sings it back to me, she slows it down, makes it sweet, almost tender.

At last the melody is not something that sounds wrong; it's not something that sounds irritating. Everything seems to fall into place.

I'm done with the flyers, so I settle in and start reading my new library book. I'm on the *M*s.

As I read, Lake keeps singing, but I realize I don't mind. I actually kind of like it. The words on the page and the words in Lake's song make me feel something. They make me feel better.

MOMMY'S LITTLE MONSTER

SOCIAL DISTORTION

Mom's voice is far away. Instead of talking about the arrangements to get home, she keeps talking about Vittorio.

I now know that Vittorio has a PhD in ancient civilizations, his specialty being moon images in ancient cultures. He is from Turin, Italy, but is a professor at the University of Madrid. He is forty-five, divorced, no kids. He can cook a gourmet meal on a Bunsen burner and is allergic to bee stings.

"He sounds OK," I say.

"He's amazing," Mom says. "I've never met anyone like him."

"You must be anxious to get home and start working on your thesis," I say.

"Well, yes, I am." She says it very slowly. "I have a new theory on domestic rituals."

"When can I book my flight home? The summer is almost over, and I don't know when I'm going home."

"Well, that's the thing, Katy. I need to write now."

"I know."

"And pretty much a person can write anywhere," she says.

"Mmm-hmm," I say.

"I really need to be away from distractions and also to be able to communicate with someone who understands my theories. Someone who was on the site."

"Right," I say. "That makes sense. Can we go shopping when I get home? I want to go to Cours Mont-Royal and get some new clothes before school starts. And I want to eat some *poutine*. Do you know you can't get cheese curds in the U.S.? Crazy, eh?"

"Well, Katy, Vittorio has invited me to go to Madrid with him to continue work on my thesis because he has to go back to get ready for school."

"What does that mean?"

"Well, it means that I'm on a roll."

"But school starts in two weeks," I say. "I have to get ready. I have to go home."

"I know, I know. But there's a great international high school in Madrid. You can start there in three weeks. Won't that be amazing? It's going to be such a great cultural opportunity for you."

The floor has dropped out from under me.

"Now?" I say. "*Now* you want me to have a cultural experience?"

"Just think, you'll be surrounded by a two-thousand-year-old city!"

I wanted to go to the rain forest. I wanted to be on the dig. I wanted to shower outside. I wanted to live in a tent. I don't want to go to Madrid. I want to go home to Montréal.

I know what's going on. *Vittorio.* She's in love with him.

I could have stopped this whole love affair with Vittorio if I had gone to Peru. Mom wouldn't have forgotten about her responsibilities to me. What did The Rat call being on tour? Unreal. A dream. Adventure time. She is just on adventure time. This Vittorio thing can't be real. She's dreaming. She's not being realistic.

Going to Madrid for a guy is stupid.

"You're going to give up your place at McGill for *Vittorio*?" I say. "You're going to do that for a man? I thought you said that a woman never does stuff like that. A woman should be independent."

"First of all, I *am* independent," my mother says, her tone more serious. "Second of all, we live in the twenty-first century. I'm writing my thesis. I'll be in correspondence with my advisor at McGill."

"You're moving for a guy."

"I'm moving because the man that I am doing my research with lives in Madrid, and I want to be with him. The distance was going to be a complication, so I eliminated it."

She says it so simply. So matter-of-factly. So unlike the Mom I know. She's changed.

"So that's it," I say.

"Yes," she says. "We'll go to Montréal, pick up our stuff, and go to Madrid. I've already sublet the house."

All at once, I can't see straight. Tears are shooting right out of my eyeballs, and the phone has slid off my ear and is sitting limply in my palm, threatening to fall to the floor. I'm barely holding on to it when The Rat comes over and takes it out of my hand and puts the phone up to his ear.

I don't hear what he's saying into the phone to my mom. It's like I'm wearing a helmet over my head. Or I've suddenly gone deaf. And asthmatic. I can't breathe.

Suddenly The Rat is holding the phone up against my ear. And from far away I hear my mom say that everything is going to be all right and that she loves me.

I know she's a liar. She loves Vittorio *more*.

I'm still crying. I don't say anything back. And then the phone is put away and The Rat is steering me toward my bedroom and I'm blubbering. Almost screaming. And he's lying to me, too. Telling me that everything is going to be fine.

I lie on my bed and I start kicking and screaming. And it's like I'm watching myself from one million miles away, like I'm having some kind of out-of-body experience. I'm not even acting like myself. I'm acting like a two-year-old.

I start punching my pillow. I sit up and I punch the pillow. I punch and punch it.

The Rat comes into my room, standing in the doorway, watching me. And now he's punching his fists on his thighs and it makes a beat and so I start punching the pillow in time with him.

I start saying words as I punch. "Di-sas-ter. Cat-a-stroph-ic. A-poc-a-lyp-tic. Earth-shat-ter-ing. Aw-ful."

One punch per syllable.

Somehow, the rhythm relaxes me. I keep doing it until I feel worn out and tired.

I don't even get out of my clothes. I don't even get under the covers. I just lie back and hit the bed. And then I'm asleep.

When I wake up the next day, my shoes are off and the knit blanket is over me and Sid Vicious is purring next to me and the sun is streaming in through the window all happy-like and it makes me smile. But when I'm fully awake, I remember.

I'm finally going back to home to Montréal only to abandon it for Madrid.

BLANK GENERATION

RICHARD HELL

"I heard what happened," Trixie says when she opens the door.

I nod. She's whispering because Auggie is asleep.

"Well, I have to get to work. How about we talk about it when I get home?"

I nod. I don't speak. I've given up speaking. No one understands. Trixie nods back and heads out the door.

I sit on the couch. I don't turn on the TV. I don't open my book. I just stare at the wall. A scratch at the door startles me, and I let out a little yelp when it opens.

Trixie stands in the frame.

"It's bad, isn't it?" she says.

I nod.

"Fuck work. Do you want to talk?"

I nod.

"I'll put some chamomile tea on."

I sit like a zombie on the couch, being totally unhelpful, while she putters in the kitchen and then the kettle screams and then Trixie comes through the beaded curtain of La Sirena that separates the kitchen from the living room, carrying a tray with tea, cookies, a pint of ice cream, and two spoons. She puts the tray on the coffee table and sits down next to me.

"I brought out all the emergency girl-talk rations."

I lean forward and take a cookie and put it in my mouth and chew. The chocolate kind of melts in my mouth, and after I swallow, I start talking. I look straight ahead and I tell Trixie everything that I can't say to The Rat. I say things I can't say to Mom. I say things I didn't even know I felt.

"I didn't want to come here. I didn't want to be separated. I wanted to go to Peru. I was afraid that I was going to lose her. Lose our special bond. And now I have."

"You're not losing her," Trixie says.

"My mom and I are a team," I say.

"You still are."

"No, she and Vittorio are a team now."

"That's how it feels, but it's not true."

I don't want to let her get a word in edgewise, so I just open my mouth and talk.

"I don't like The Rat. I was fine without him. I didn't need him in my life. And I feel like I've had to be nice to him because he's trying so hard. And did you know that Lake was bribed all summer to be friends with me? Lake calls me Beige, because that's what I am. Boring. Bland. Beige. She doesn't even like me. No one here likes me. Except Garth. But Garth likes everyone, so that doesn't really count. And then there is Leo. I liked Leo so much and he used me. I liked Leo so much, and I hurt so much, and if Mom were here, then I could talk to her about it and she could give me advice. But I can't because she's in love and she's forgotten all about me and no one ever asked me what I wanted."

Trixie's arm comes up and goes around my shoulder and she pulls me in for a hug, and when my face reaches her shoulder, I sigh. She smells like jasmine. She strokes my hair and she says, "Katy, that's a lot to keep all bottled up inside."

I'm so glad someone can see that. Finally.

"So, what am I going to do?"

"You're going to hang in there. It's going to be all right."

"It doesn't feel like it's going to be all right. It feels like my mother is abandoning me. Like I'm not interesting to her anymore. I really am beige."

"She's not abandoning you."

"Yes, she is. She's picking a *guy* over me! I want to go *home*! And now I have to go to another new country, and this time I don't even speak the language!"

I'm totally yelling. I didn't know I could be so loud. Auggie is going to wake up for sure. Trixie doesn't seem to mind. She just lets me yell.

"Katy, she's living her life for the first time. And she can't do it without you. Think about that."

"Are you going to be like every other adult and tell me it's a great opportunity?"

"No," Trixie says. "I think it sucks. I wish Vittorio were going to move to Montréal. Make the man change his life, I say. It's such a typical gender role for the woman to have to change her life for a man."

"Yeah," I say. That hurts because it sounds like something Mom would say.

"You know, Katy, your mom is really young," Trixie says.

"I know."

"I mean, she's ten years younger than I am."

"No."

"Yeah. You know what I was doing when I was in my twenties and thirties?" Trixie asks. "I was making big mistakes and dating the wrong guy. And getting out of a stupid marriage. And I was wild. And I was independent. And I did whatever I wanted. I went crazy and did crazy things and I was selfish. You know what your mom was doing? None of that. She had you."

"She probably regrets it now," I say.

"I doubt it. You know, you're not so far from the age she was when she had you," Trixie says.

I stop. I am nearly fifteen. And Mom was

eighteen. I try to imagine having my own baby three years from now. I can't. It seems impossible. I would never be able to do it.

That makes me cry again. It must have been so hard.

"Don't you see?" Trixie says. "Your mom and I are kind of opposite, you know. Now I am in my forties and I have Auggie, and my whole life has changed. I can't do anything that I used to do. And that's really hard. I have had to make a lot of sacrifices. But I'm happy to do it. I'm ready. Just like your mom was when she had you. You're old enough to be your own person now. She's just letting loose a little."

"But I don't want anything to change," I say, and—I can't help it—I start crying harder. Trixie hands me a Kleenex, 'cause I've got snot bubbles coming out of my nose.

"She might be ready for a change, but I'm not."

"Ah, sweet Katy, nothing ever stays the same," Trixie says. "The only thing you can take care of is yourself and how you feel. You can only make the best of it."

I want to tell her that I can't bear the idea of

spending years in Madrid wishing I were home. Just like I spent the whole summer in L.A. pretending I was somewhere else.

I'm so not depressed anymore.

I'm angry.

EVERYTHING SUCKS

THE DESCENDENTS

We are dropping off the flyers at Amoeba Records for the Grown-Ups' warm-up show at Skooby's Hot Dogs.

"So, wait. You're moving to *Spain*?" Lake says.

"Yeah, I'm going to go to an international school there."

"Too bad you still don't *habla español*," she says.

I slam the pile of flyers down on the counter.

"Could you just not do that?" I say.

"Not do what?"

"Pick on me and make me feel worse about my already horrible situation," I say.

"Well, it's true!" Lake says.

I shoot her a look.

"So what *should* I say?"

"How about 'That sucks.' Or 'Good luck.' Or 'Whoa. Bummer.'"

"OK, I hear you," Lake says. "It *is* a bummer."

I thought we were just going in and out, but Lake pulls me deeper into the store and starts browsing. I don't know what to do here. I'm standing in the aisles surrounded by rows and rows of CDs.

The clicking of the plastic as people flip through the discs starts to have a soothing effect on me. It's got a rhythm. It must lull everyone else, too. All around me, people are concentrated and dreamy-looking as they flip. It's so Zen.

A song comes onto the speaker. It startles me. I know it.

The boy next to me, flipping through the racks, glances at me and nods in approval. As though I'm in the know.

I *am* in the know.

It's Suck.

Sam's voice is screaming through the speaker. I look around. Nobody is panicking. Some people's heads are bobbing up and down in time.

I check myself. I'm fine. I'm not panicking. It's not making me crazy. It's not taking me anywhere I don't want to go.

I head toward *S*. Suck has its own divider.

Then I start looking for all the bands on Garth's mix CD. I pull the CDs out and examine the covers.

"Did you find something?" Lake says, pulling the CDs out of my hand.

I nod. I did find something.

"Huh," she says. "Not bad."

U. SUCK A. /
WE'RE FED UP

SCREAM

I hear The Rat talking on the phone. I can hear him through the open window. He thinks he's being clever 'cause he's stepped outside, like he is going to smoke a cigarette or something. But he's not being clever.

He's coming in loud and clear. He's talking about me.

"Is she upset? How would I know?" he says. "Right now she's kind of always upset."

It's true. I am upset at everything.

"That's true—I remember my teen years. Kind of."

Then he laughs.

"I'm glad that she's been here, because it's about making up for lost time. But now Suck wants to go on tour," The Rat says. "Two months is a long time."

I move away from the window so I won't have to listen to him, but he's still coming in loud and clear.

"Yeah. I guess I'm ready for her to leave. It's going to be kind of nice to be selfish again."

I forget to breathe. Everybody is ready for me to leave. Everybody is ready to forget about me.

I know what I need to do. I need to leave *first*. Who am I kidding? I would never do that. I couldn't. I'm just not that kind of girl. I just don't have that much rebel in me. But my body starts moving. My hand is turning the knob.

Instead of just thinking about it, I do it. I head out the front door.

My feet hit the pavement hard. I feel it through the bottom of my brand-new Chuck Taylors. My pace quickens. It's dark, and nobody walks in L.A.

I push the gate open and head down the driveway. I stand on my tippy toes and feel behind the wing of the angel. I got it. The spare key to the jam space.

I open the door and then lock it up behind me. I flick on the lamps and get a good vibe going. At last I can let it all out. In here it doesn't feel stupid to cry or scream. This jam space is the only place to go.

The instruments seem to beckon to me. But no matter how hard they try, I'm not tempted to bang on the drums—even though a part of me knows deep down inside that banging on them will probably make me feel better. I don't want to feel better. I pull out the blanket and lie down on the couch.

"Oh, thank God."

Through crusty eyes I see The Rat standing above me. Lake is standing next to him.

"I told you," she says. "Nothing to worry about."

It must be like four in the morning.

"Do you know how worried I was about you? Don't you ever do that again!" he yells.

"Do what?"

"Run away! You do not have permission to run away."

"I thought you said by the time you were my age, you'd run away like five times, gotten a tattoo, been kicked out of three bands, and had sex."

"That's different."

"How?"

"It just is."

"It's not different."

"You're different, Katy," The Rat says. "I thank God you're different than me."

"I wanted to be alone."

"You could have gone to Trixie's." He takes off his cowboy hat and rubs his head.

"I told you she'd be here," Lake says, piping up from the doorway. "And it's no wonder. I'd be pissed off if I were Beige, too."

"Lake, please stay out of this," The Rat says.

"Rat, be a little more grateful," Lake says. "I showed you where she was."

"And I thank you for it," The Rat says.

"I can take care of myself," I say. "I didn't do anything stupid. I just had to get out of the house."

"That's not a good enough reason to run away," he says.

I bet he's run away for stupider reasons in his

time. I can tell that he hates that he sounds like a parent, but I know he has to say it.

"If I'm different, don't you trust me?" I ask him.

"I do."

"If you trusted me, you'd know that I would have come home tomorrow like a good little girl and packed my stuff up to go to Madrid," I say.

"But now you've broken the trust. I can't trust you when you leave without a word."

"*I* can't trust *you*."

"Yes, you can," The Rat says.

"I *heard* you. I heard you say you were ready for me to leave. I heard you say that two months was a long time. Well, you got off pretty easy, don't you think? Two months out of fifteen years?"

"Katy, you misunderstood me. When you say it like that it does sound awful."

"It *is* awful," I say.

"Yeah, it's pretty awful," Lake says.

"Lake, shut up. I can speak for myself."

Lake looks kind of surprised. She throws her arms up in mock surrender.

"You didn't hear what I said on the phone, right," The Rat says.

"Yes, I did."

"No," he says. "You didn't hear the full context of the conversation. I was talking to Frank about how I'm going on tour in the fall for two months. I'm going to be on the road all that time. I meant that I need to be selfish and completely focused if Suck wants to make it this time."

It doesn't even register.

"I didn't *want* to come to Los Angeles. I didn't *want* to meet you again. I hate it here!"

"Katy, I want to talk about this," The Rat says.

"I'm a bother. Now you can have your life back. I'm going to be out of your way and in Mom's way."

"It's not true!" he says. "You're not in anyone's way. I love having you around!"

The Rat doesn't have anything else to say. He just rubs his face with his hands, like he's tired. I'm tired, too.

I'm so tired.

"You know what? Go away. Just let me sleep," I say.

"I'm not letting you sleep here."

"Have you ever slept in a jam space, Rat?" I ask.

"Yeah, I had to live in one for three months when I couldn't afford an apartment."

"So I can stay here for one night."

I pull my blanket up and roll over, away from him. He kind of stands there for a while and then he finally leaves me the hell alone.

SONIC REDUCER

DEAD BOYS

I let myself in, not knowing if The Rat is going to be home or not. I just want to go straight to my room. I didn't want to come home yet, but I was feeling kind of bad about being away.

The Rat is sitting on the couch working on a model airplane stretched out in front of him.

"Whoa! It's hot," The Rat says, glancing up at me.

He doesn't say, I'm glad you're home, or anything about last night. I think he's trying to be cool. He stops working and goes into the kitchen.

When he comes back, he's cracking open one of his nonalcoholic beers.

"Where's my beer?" I ask.

"You can't drink beer," he says. "You're under twenty-one."

"You can't drink beer either," I say. "You're sober."

"It's an O'Doul's. It's nonalcoholic," he says. "I like the taste."

"Me, too," I say.

I go to the kitchen and I grab myself an O'Doul's, sit down on the couch next to The Rat, and throw my legs up on the table. The bottle feels cold in my hand.

We kind of stare at each other for a minute, waiting for the other one to say something. I kind of want him to say something. I want to go ballistic. I've been extra quiet for so long. I put the bottle to my lips. It smells skunky.

The Rat sits back down on the couch.

"You know it's genetic. You're susceptible to becoming an addict because of me and your mom," The Rat says, cringing.

"A cold fake beer on a dry, hot day sometimes is the only thing that hits the spot. Isn't that what you said?"

"Yeah," he says. "It sure does."

He nods. Takes a swig.

I take a swig.

It hits the spot.

I let out a sigh.

"It's not like I haven't tried a beer before. I had one a week ago at a party with Lake."

"I remember," The Rat says. "Do you want to talk about this thing with your mom and moving to Spain?"

"No," I say.

"Do you want to talk about running away last night?"

"No."

"Do you promise that the next time we have a problem, we'll talk about what's going on?"

I don't say anything.

"I'm going to take that as a yes," The Rat says. "Do you want to be mad right now?"

"Yes."

"OK, I understand that," The Rat says. "Do you have to take it out on me?"

I don't answer him. I take another sip of near-beer.

"OK. Cool. I understand. It's OK if you do want to take it out on me. But I'm not the bad guy here."

I tap a beat out with my fingernails on the bottle. *Clink. Clink. Clink.*

KICK OUT THE JAMS
MC5

Skooby's has a little PA system on the sidewalk under the half awning, separate from the seating area. Sam Suck got roped into driving us to the show, because no one in the Grown-Ups has her driver's license yet. I sit there on a stool with Sam, minding the merch table while the Grown-Ups play.

I know their set list by heart from sitting in on their jams.

CHARMER ALARM
POLITICS OF THE HEART
ONE, TWO, THREE, WHORE!
BIOLOGY CLASS RIP

NEEDLE DICK
SUN SCREAM
MAMA'S BOY
MÉNAGE À TROIS
TINY HEART

I see Garth, kind of skulking in the background. I wave for him to come and join us. He kind of shakes his head. I leave him alone. He knows he's welcome at the table, and I see that knowing that puts a smile on his face.

Sam bobs his head up and down to the music. The guy who owns Skooby's knows exactly who Sam Suck is and gives us our hot dogs for free even though we're not in the band. He asks Sam Suck for his autograph.

"Does everybody know who you are?" I ask.

"I started Suck with The Rat in junior high so we could get girls," Sam says. "Now I get free hot dogs."

Well, that's a perk, I think.

I catch Sam looking at me. "Now you *really* remind me of your mom," he says. "When I first met her, she was *our* merch girl."

"I'm just doing this as a favor," I say.

"Funny," Sam says. "That's what your mom said, too."

I think about how my mother followed The Rat to California. Now she's following Vittorio to Madrid.

It's just like she always says: *Plus ça change, plus c'est la même chose.*

The set is almost over. They're going to end with the new song. But instead of being their usual full-on wall of sound, they strip it down. Lake sings it. Pretty. Like in the jam space. She does not growl. She sings. And the other girls hang back and don't add too much more to the song. They keep it the way I liked it, when Lake was singing it just for me.

> *"It's been*
> *three days*
> *still haven't*
> *heard from you.*
>
> *My heart*
> *lives underwater*
> *breathing for you.*

But you
break apart
my tiny heart,
giving me
no chance to start
something
with you.

I dove into the pool
I dove in
hoping to swim
now I'm drowning."

I never really listened to the words in a song before this. When the words are right, they make you sad and happy at the same time. Because you know, you just know, that what's being said is true. You feel like the song was written just for you. And in this case, I guess it really was.

I get goose bumps as I listen to Lake singing it *my way*. I start to sing along in my head.

GROUP SEX

CIRCLE JERKS

Garth stands there at the edge of the pool, more bones than skin. He sticks his arms out in an Arnold Schwarzenegger man-of-iron pose. It looks ridiculous. But he has everyone at the pool laughing. He keeps hamming it up.

Lake sits on the lounge chair with her big sun hat and her composition notebook, scribbling away.

I keep on the lookout for Leo. I keep staring at his balcony. I can't help it. Even though he never really liked me.

I try not to cry.

Lake starts humming and mouthing words. I watch her lips part to show perfect teeth in the form of a smile. She smiles when she's coming up with a song.

Garth has stopped jumping around playing with his non-muscles. I notice that he's kind of standing there, leaning in, trying to listen to Lake's half singing.

I notice something else.

Garth doesn't have a boner anymore.

"Is that the kind of girl you like? Lake?" I ask Garth later at the gelato store.

"I dunno."

"You don't know?"

"Well. OK. Yeah. But . . ."

"She wasn't flirting with you when she asked you to go up to my house to get a new pen for her."

"I know. I'm still making progress with her. But maybe she'll talk to me this year at school. What do you think?"

"Probably not," I say. "Sorry, Garth."

"I wish you were going to be here," Garth says. "You make things bearable."

"She wasn't even flirting when she asked you to stop by the jam space tomorrow to help her," I say. "She's just using you."

"I know." Garth nods to himself. "I know she doesn't like me, and anything that I think that might be happening with her is just in my head. But at least she asked me to help at Sunset Junction."

I keep my mouth shut. It hits a bit too close to home. A bit too close to how I felt about Leo. Leo, who I've made about one hundred excuses for to explain his bad behavior. Leo, who I've tried to convince myself is still thinking about that night as much as I am even though he told me to my face that it meant nothing.

"What makes her hot?" I ask. "What makes a girl like Lake hot?"

"The way she moves. The way she looks. The way she wears her clothes," Garth says. "The way she's got stuff on her mind. The way she's totally independent. The way she doesn't want me."

"I wonder if I'll ever be that hot."

"Sure. You are now. I mean not to me. But you know what I mean."

"I probably need more boobs, though. Lake has big boobs."

"She sure does," Garth says kind of dreamy.

I want to laugh at him, because he's acting like

a girl, not just looking like one. Then I do it. I open my mouth and laugh right out loud.

"Thanks, Garth. I needed that."

"Hey, man," he says, "anytime."

We walk back into the courtyard, and I hear laughing. My eyes glance up toward Leo's. I see him come out on his balcony. He's with someone. I hear giggling. He pulls a girl out onto the balcony. She's protesting, like she doesn't want to go out, but she kind of does.

He looks down in the courtyard and sees me, then he pulls the girl close to him and wraps his arms around her. He sees me watching him, but I don't let him see that it bothers me. I don't give him the satisfaction. Instead, I smile and wave.

I look up at my nails. Lake's black nail polish looks good on them.

NO WAY

ADOLESCENTS

The Sunset Junction Street Fair is today, a whole day of rides and games and booths, right in my front yard. Except I can't explore. I said I was going to help Lake. I sit on the side of the stage and wait until Lake shows up.

"Where's Garth?" Lake asks.

"I'm not his babysitter," I say.

"He said he'd be here."

"Well then, he'll be here," I say.

"Go find a table and set up the stuff," Lake says. "You have to set up the merch. That's your job."

"I thought my job was lugging all your equipment."

"It's called 'loading in,'" Lake says. "That's why I need Garth."

"Where is your band?" I ask.

"They don't do the hard work," Lake says. "I have to make it easy for them or they won't do stuff, like show up."

Right. Easy on them. Hard on me.

I get it when I see them. The other girls are talking to boys. They aren't interested in the nitty-gritty of being in a band. Just the glory. That's why I helped with the flyers. That's why I'm moving the boxes and boxes of merch.

I am too sweaty to keep working like a dog. I'm hot and bored and tired. I didn't want to be a mover. One of the boxes falls off the table and Lake glares at me. I throw my arms up in the air. It's not my fault there is just too much stuff. It's annoying.

Garth finally skates up to us a big smile on his face, helmet firmly on his head, and an ice-cream cone in his hand.

"Where have you been?" Lake asks. "You're late."

"No, I'm not. You told me to get here at quarter of." He lifts his wristwatch to show us that he's on time. "Let's get this merch organized."

Garth hands me his ice-cream cone, which I start eating, and he starts to prettify the merch table. He could be an interior decorator, he's got such an artistic eye.

The Grown-Ups get up on stage and start to sound-check. All Lake does is complain. Everything is a problem. The drums don't sound right. Her vocals don't sound right. Her guitar doesn't sound right. The other girls' backups don't sound right.

It all sounds fine to me. Her problem is she's a perfectionist, maybe.

The sun is hot, hot, hot. I am hungry and want to explore the street fair. It's just opening up for the day, not too crowded. Not yet. I want to ride on the rides. I want to buy something cute. I might as well buy something L.A. that I can wear in Madrid.

When Lake joins us, she's muttering. She's mad as hell, while the other girls in the band all hang out together on the other side of the stage, giggling. Not helping.

"Poseurs," Lake says.

"What? Who?"

"The rest of the band. They are poseurs."

She's saying this to me, the biggest poseur of them all. What am I doing here?

The fair is starting to get more crowded. Some of the people head straight for the merch table, make a beeline for me. Lake kind of pushes me and Garth out of the way and takes over, telling everyone what is what. Bullying them into buying stuff. She starts handing me the wads of cash.

"How much is the the Grown-Ups underwear?" a boy asks.

"Five dollars," Lake says. She grabs the twenty out of the boy's hand, and I quietly make change, glad for something to do.

"Perv," she says as he leaves. And we laugh.

A stagehand comes over to the table and alerts Lake that it's almost set time. Kids and adults start to gather by the stage, waiting for the Grown-Ups, which is the first band to go on.

"Beige is in charge of the store," Lake says to Garth. "Help her, lame-o."

Then she blows over to the backstage area and disappears.

In between selling the odd piece of merch, I can observe the Junction with a purpose. My eyes scan the crowd, noticing all the kids. I see Auggie on top of The Rat's shoulders with food all over his face. Trixie is laughing. People are having a good time.

My eyes are drawn to someone flying out of the gated-off backstage area. It's Lake, followed by the other girls in the band. They're yelling. Oh, no. This is not good. Lake disappears out of my range of view and then emerges with her guitar. She then comes pushing through the crowd toward me.

"Let's go!" she yells.

I'm confused. I can't move.

"Katy. Now. Come."

I don't know why I should come with her. I don't know what's happened. I do know that she's called me *Katy*. Not Beige.

"Garth, stay here for me, OK?" I say.

"Anything for you, Beige."

I grab my stuff and I follow her out into the crowd before she can disappear from view.

We walk three blocks through the thickening crowd and I'm practically running behind her. I want to stop for kettle corn or sausage or a *papusa* or an iced tea. But I can't. I want to know what's happened.

"What's going on?" I say, out of breath, finally

catching up to her stride. "Aren't you on in like fifteen minutes?"

"I kicked those bitches out."

"What?"

"They called me a friggin' band Nazi," Lake says. She stops walking. She looks right at me. "I just want to be good. I don't need them. I told them they could find a new band after the show, but they bailed."

She sounds like a cartoon. A mad, angry cartoon. I don't know where we are going. She sits down on the curb. She puts her head in her hands. She starts to cry. Blubbery. Sobbing. Heartbroken.

"This was my big chance," Lake says. "This is where it was all going to start for me."

If she were my friend, I might know what to say.

Wait a minute. Lake *is* my friend. I *do* know what to say.

I stand up.

Who am I kidding? What I have to say is crazy.

I sit back down. I look at Lake. Her shoulders are slumped. She looks defeated. She looks nothing like the Lake I know. Running away. Not singing. It's so very . . . beige.

There can't be two of us. I take her hand in mine.

"Come on," I say. "You have a show to play."

"What? Didn't you hear me? I have no band."

She just needs to know she can do it. I'm the only one who knows she can.

"You have your guitar," I say.

"Play by myself? *No way.*"

"Sing all your songs stripped down, like 'Tiny Heart.' Like you did at Skooby's. It sounded really good," I say.

She shakes her head no.

"I can't."

"Are you scared?" I ask.

Lake looks at me.

That's it. Lake-the-Fearless is scared. She's not so different from me. I know all about being scared. But I also know that Lake is supposed to rock today. There's only one thing to do. Leap to her rescue.

"I'll sing backup."

"Can you sing?" she asks.

"I don't know," I say. "Probably not."

Lake's sobbing changes to laughter. "That's the stupidest idea *ever*," she says.

Then that little feeling I had of being sure just kind of pops, like a soap bubble. "Yeah, I know," I say.

"But Beige, you're a genius!" She jumps up and grabs me.

We run back through the street fair to the stage.

"What's going on?" Garth asks as we whiz by.

"Keep minding the store," I say. He salutes me.

And then Lake and I climb up on the stage.

There are a lot more people in front of us than I thought. People of all sorts. Young, old, regular, normal, punks. It's a lot of people. I've never really been on stage before. I'll be useless up here. I lied to Lake. I mean, really, who am I kidding? I can't do this. I catch her eye. I see that she's still scared. It's too late to back out now. So I just nod encouragingly.

She nods back. Looking determined. She straps her guitar on and flips a switch.

"Hi, I'm Lake Suck, and this is my girl, Beige. And we're here to rock."

People are just kind of standing around looking

at us quizzically, except Garth. Garth is standing on top of the merch table, whistling and clapping.

Oh, God. I'm going to throw up.

I look down at the set list. The first song is "Charmer Alarm."

OK. I know it. I totally know it. I open my mouth at the right spots. It is weird, hearing my voice amplified by the microphone. Actually it confuses me, so I try to forget about the voice that is out there being amplified and concentrate on the one inside my head. Lake keeps singing but looks back over at me and flashes me a smile and waves for me to sing louder.

I'm glad she doesn't seem nervous anymore. But I am. I'm sweating bullets.

I close my eyes for a second to situate myself. I try to listen for her guitar. It sounds almost different up on the stage. But it's loud. OK. That's coming from the monitor. I hear the melody. The melody that makes sense to me. I just try to remember what the other girls sang in the song. I know this. I can do this. I open my eyes and I listen for the spots that need some support. I make my voice do something just a teensy bit different at the chorus. It might not sound as good, but

Lake is still singing. I hear myself in the monitor. Just breathe. Just wait. Just go. Just sing.

When I sing the words, Lake's words, it's like I know her a little bit better. It makes me proud of her, that she can express herself this way. It's like everything she can't say like a normal person she can say in a song. And we're singing it together.

Then the song is done. Lake hits the chords to the next one.

I look down at the set list. "One, Two, Three, Whore!"

Oh, yeah. I know a good part that I can do. I can double her scream. Yeah. That'll sound good. It'll feel good, too.

I just keep listening for the music to tell me where to open my mouth.

Halfway through the set, I look up. I'm surprised to see the crowd sticking around. They are enjoying the show. They are clapping.

There's this kind of energy that moves between me on the stage and the people out in the crowd. It's a flow. I feel buzzy inside. And proud, like I'm doing something right.

I see Garth whistling from the merch booth. I see Sam Suck hooting and hollering. Trixie is in the back, smiling, kind of moving her body in time to the music with Auggie in her arms. I see The Rat standing next to her with an astonished look on his face.

We don't sound half bad.

For the next song, I sing a little bit louder.

SOUND AND FURY

YOUTH BRIGADE

"Wow! Just WOW!" Garth says. "That was the baddest-ass show ever!"

"Did we sell stuff?" Lake asks.

"Yeah," Garth says. "People just swarmed me."

Sam Suck comes up to us to offer his congratulations.

"That has a lot of potential, I think," he says. "Lake, I think you can go a little sparser with the guitar if you don't have the backup band."

"OK. OK, Dad, give me a break. I haven't figured it out yet," Lake says. She sounds like she's bugged, but I know she's not. I can tell that she's excited. She's thinking. She's working it out for herself. She's itching to keep going in this new direction. I don't know how I can tell, except that I do.

Maybe because I feel so good.

The Rat grabs me from behind in a bear hug and swings me around.

"My, my, my, my, my!" The Rat says. "My, oh, my!"

"That was something else, Katy," Trixie says. "I think your dad is trying to tell you that he liked it."

The Rat just looks at me, all beaming. All smiling. All excited. I don't want him to make a big deal out of it. He's making me blush.

"How do you feel, kiddo?" he says.

"All right," I say. I shrug. I withhold. I'm not ready to share just yet. I need to think for a minute. Sort out my feelings.

I still need to digest it all. I need to keep the buzz going on for a minute so I can sort it out. But I want to say, *I FELT TERRIFIC! HOLY, HOLY! WHEN I WAS ON STAGE, I FELT COMPLETELY ALIVE! DO YOU FEEL THAT?*

"Cool, yeah. I could picture like a real minimal beat behind it, but you know it doesn't need it," The Rat says, kind of toning down his enthusiasm a bit, kind of getting that I need to reflect on what I just did up there.

"I don't know. I don't know anything," I say. "I was just helping Lake."

"Right, right," The Rat says. But he's still beaming. "Yeah, of course, you were helping out a friend."

A friend. Yes. Lake is my friend.

The Rat doesn't say too much more, and I'm happy about that. I just want to feel it. I'm kind of floating around while Lake is jumping up and down with happiness.

"I wish you'd told me what you girls were up to," Sam says. "Next time, I'll record you off the soundboard so you can hear it."

Next time?

Lake and I wander the booths and ride the rides and check out the crowds. There are all sorts here. *All* sorts. Dressed up in wigs. In leather. In rainbows. With colored eyebrows and shaved heads. I eat one of everything. I ride every ride. I sit on the curb.

All day I bask in the glow of the after-show. It feels so good. I didn't know it felt this good to perform. I feel ten feet tall. I feel terrific. I feel like I can conquer the world. I buy a funky orange skirt, a skirt for the new me. Lake helps me pick it out. I feel strong and a bit cocky in an *I-am-Lake* way.

No. In an *I-am-Beige* way.

Last on the bill is Suck. I thought it was crowded earlier, but when Suck takes the stage, it is crazy.

Lake grabs my hand and pulls me all the way to the front so we lean forward on the stage. When Suck comes on, everyone starts screaming.

I watch Sam as he jumps around and pushes himself off of the monitors. I watch the bass player and The Rat on the drum riser. He's like an animal, even more explosive than at the Fourth of July party. People are screaming the lyrics. Screaming them.

I kind of get it. I get the way they move; they are forced that way by the way the guitars chug and by the attack of the drums. You'd have to ride on the notes that way. You'd have to. I watch The Rat as he bangs away. He's just grabbing what's given and throwing it back out.

I close my eyes. I'm still riding the buzz from

my own show. Even though the music and words sound dangerous, I know they're not. I wouldn't go there. I am more interested in my heart. But I am starting to understand why *they* do.

I open my eyes and see The Rat.

There's that connection again, a string that moves from me, to him, to his drums. I relax. I let the rhythm enter me. My body starts to sway. I bob my head in time to The Rat's drumming.

The Rat sees me in the crowd. He's looking at me. He's smiling at me. The crowd behind me, the kids, the middle-aged, the old around me, sing along. They jump and move around. They are moved by the music.

And, in my own way, so am I.

GERM FREE ADOLESCENTS

X-RAY SPEX

After returning all my books to the Los Feliz Library, I meet Garth at the Casbah. We don't say much. We just kind of drink our coffee and stare out the window. It's kind of hard to say anything.

"Well," I say finally. "I should go. The Rat said we're having a *bon voyage* dinner."

"Cool," he says. "I'll walk you home."

We walk slowly and I take in all the now-familiar sights on Sunset. I even say good-bye to that Walking Man, although he just walks right by me, too busy talking on his cell phone.

When we get to my door, Garth starts blinking like crazy.

"Are you OK?" I ask.

"I got some dust in my eye," he says. "Stupid wind."

But I know there's no dust and that he's really crying because he's sensitive, and I like that about him. Thinking about not hanging out with Garth every day makes me get a little choked up, so I put on the vintage cat-eye sunglasses that Lake gave me as a going-away present so that anything that might come leaking out of my eyes won't be seen.

"OK, bye, then," I say.

"Bye, Beige."

And then we kind of stand there. I look at the ground. Then I look at a palm tree. And then Garth pulls me in roughly for a hug. And we hug for a minute and his skateboard is kind of digging into my back and his helmet is pressing too hard against my cheek, but I don't care. When we break apart, Garth puts his board on the ground and just skates away.

When I get up to the apartment, The Rat is MIA. I find a note on my bed that says, *Dinner, Trixie's, 6 p.m. — Formal Wear.*

One thing I know for sure: if Trixie says dress for dinner, she means really dress for dinner.

I put my new skirt on, and at first I'm not sure it's right for me. Maybe it's too wild. But as I check myself out in the mirror, I think I look kind of good.

I open the door to Trixie's and take in the scene. She's painted a big *bon voyage* sign, which she's hung with a bunch of vintage decorations in the living room. On the dining table, under the glass, is a poster of Madrid.

Auggie comes running up to me to give me a hug. He's wearing a tiny little tuxedo. Trixie finishes setting the table, and she looks amazing in a black chiffon cocktail dress from the fifties with her hair done in an upsweep.

The room smells delicious.

The Rat comes out of the kitchen wearing his best suit and a skinny black tie. He's got one of Trixie's frilly aprons on.

"You're the guest of honor, so you sit at the head of the table," he says. Then he disappears back into the kitchen. I sit down and so does Trixie, who's put Auggie into his chair.

A few minutes later, The Rat comes out of the kitchen proudly holding a platter. He sets it on the table.

It's a roast. He cooked me a roast. My favorite.

"Open your present," Trixie says, pointing to the envelope sitting on my plate.

"OK," I say. The Rat makes a drumroll on the table as I tear it open.

"It's a voucher for a plane ticket," Trixie explains. "You can use it to go wherever you want."

"But of course, we hope you might come back and visit," The Rat says. "Just give me some notice so I can clean the place up before you get here."

"And if The Rat is still on tour, you can always stay with me," Trixie says, passing the rosemary roasted potatoes.

I don't know what to say.

I look at Trixie, The Rat, and Auggie surrounding me as they meet my eyes when I look up.

They look like a family.

Wait.

They look like *my* family.

SPELLBOUND

SIOUXSIE AND THE BANSHEES

After dinner, I go back to my room and pack up my bags. I don't have to pack everything. I am supposed to be paring down.

There's nothing that I want to keep from this bedroom anyway. My eyes scan the room to make sure. They fall on the purple guitar, sitting in its stand in the corner next to the desk.

I walk over and touch it.

The strings squeak as I move my hands along the fret board. The squeak mixes nicely in the air. The squeak reminds me of Lake. And Garth. And Leo. And Trixie. And The Rat. And I feel sad. Sad that I'm leaving.

On the desk I notice Lake's Sharpie pen. I pick it up and uncap it.

I stand up on my bed and face the wall. I begin to write.

My name is Beige Ratner Bernier, and this is my manifesto. I was born in Hell. But I am no demon. I am beige and colorful. I was quiet in this room. But I am learning to be loud. Can you hear me? I will make my mark, wherever I am. It is my space. I'll make it mine. I choose. I choose. If I voice my truth, no one loses.

I hear The Rat's key in the door. I jump off my bed. I don't have to turn back and survey what I've written because it's not finished. I have more words to write down. But for now, it's time to go.

SHOULD I STAY OR SHOULD I GO

THE CLASH

We don't say much on the ride to the airport. The Rat tap-tap-taps out a beat. I can't stand it. I break down. I turn the radio on.

"*. . . that was the punk news—glad to bring it to youse.*"

The guitars start, then the others join in, then the drum kicks in. I know this song. I know it and I like it. It's the Clash.

The Rat, still beating away at the steering wheel, opens his mouth and starts to sing, and then I start singing, and we are singing together.

I turn the volume up as loud as it goes.

I sing at the top of my lungs. I scream, scream, scream the song. The Rat duets with me, singing the guitar parts and the Spanish parts. We're blasting down the highway, going just five miles above the speed limit, but it feels so fast. I roll down the windows and sing to the passing cars on the freeway. The sun is shining, the way it almost always seems to in Los Angeles, just a perfect blue cloudless sunny day. And the palm trees are swaying, like they are dancing to a rhythm they've made up all by themselves.

I am happy and sad at the same time.

It's only a minute, but I want it to last forever. And then it's over and we're there.

We pull up to the parking lot at LAX. A new song has started on the radio. The moment in the car is over. We get out in silence. Don't talk much. The Rat carries my luggage, and I'm finally on my way to Montréal, even if it is just to leave again.

Bags checked, I clutch my carry-on. Nervous. The Rat walks me to the TSA security check. The security checkpoint will separate us.

"You have everything?" he asks.

"Yeah," I say.

"Here's a twenty in case you want some coffee or candy or a magazine."

I take the twenty. I mumble a thank-you.

He looks down at his grungy Chuck Taylors. Then he looks back up at me. His eyes are kind of watery. He purses his lips.

"It was really great having you here, Katy. It was no trouble at all. Come back anytime. I want you to come back. *Mi casa es tu casa.*"

"Yeah, OK," I say, but I kind of whisper it because I have to bite the inside of my cheeks. There's a weight on my chest suddenly and my throat feels tight.

"Where's your guitar?" he asks.

"It's back in my room," I manage to say. "Will you keep it tuned and ready for me?"

The Rat pulls me into one of his big bear hugs. I smell the cigarettes and the near-beer and the BO, and I don't mind it. It smells like The Rat and I'll miss it. I don't want to be rid of him.

I can't speak now. I can't say anything, not even good-bye. I just reach into my bag and pull out my boarding pass, hoping to distract myself as I walk away. But I can't.

I turn around. The Rat is still standing there. He's actually crying. He doesn't care that anybody is watching him as he's watching me go.

And then I start to cry, too.

"DAD!" I call.

He looks surprised. "What is it?"

"Rock on!" I yell.

He smiles. And flips me the thumbs-up.

I step through the metal detector.

I've made up my mind. I'm off to Madrid. But really, I'm on my way.

I'm on *my* way.

MERCI BEAUCOUP:

Everyone I ever played music with—
especially Julie McGovern, Nancy Ross,
and Kim Temple;

my friends and gentle readers—Cylin Busby,
Mette Ivie Harrison, Jo Knowles, and
Lauren Myracle;

Rachel Cohn—for lending me a laptop;

Liza Palmer—coffeehouse study buddy;

Holly Black—for a room to write in, a shoulder
to cry on, and all things magical;

Joseph Brady—for coining phrases that
make my heart sing;

Steve Salardino—as always;

Jennifer Laughran, Not Your Mother's Book Club
and Books, Inc.;

Kerry Slattery and Skylight Books
for constant support;

my Candlewick peeps—especially Deb Wayshak;

Barry "Mr. Fantastic" Goldblatt—
and all the members of Camp Barry;

and to the divine Ms. Kara LaReau—who is every
color of the rainbow—this one is for you.